THE NEWCOMER

Pony Club Series

The Newcomer

Diane Redmond

Illustrations by Linda Boddy

Hodder
Children's
Books

a division of Hodder Headline plc

First published in Great Britain in 1995
by Hodder Children's Books

A Catalogue record for this book is available from the British Library

ISBN 0-340-62649-6

Typeset by Avon Dataset Ltd, Bidford-on-Avon, B50 4JH

Printed and bound in Great Britain by
Cox & Wyman Ltd, Reading, Berks.

Hodder Children's Books
A Division of Hodder Headline plc
338 Euston Road
London NW1 3BH

For Amy and Lucas, himself.

Contents

Chapter One

Wit's End

As the removal van thundered down the M25 and London became a grey blur on the horizon, Polly leant back in the seat of her mum's battered old estate car and sighed with relief. At long, long last they were on the move. Catching her daughter's expression in the wing mirror, Lizzie Styles held up one hand to show her crossed fingers.

'A new life,' she said. 'Let's hope it's a happy one.'

'Oh, it will be, mum,' Polly answered quickly.

Lizzie smiled at her daughter's tumbled

auburn curls falling carelessly over her small heart-shaped face. Her bright blue eyes, normally brimming with life and enthusiasm, were brooding and rather thoughtful. For a ten year old kid she'd been through quite a bit over the last few months. So had Sam, her big brother, thought Mrs Styles, firmly fixing her attention on the traffic in front of her. There couldn't have been two more different children. Four years older than his sister, Sam was big and bulky where Polly was small and wiry. Sam didn't share his sister's sizzling vitality. He was quiet and withdrawn, preferring his music to people, while she was a laughing extrovert, liking nothing more than a big crowd and plenty of action. Mrs Styles wondered how both of them would cope with country life after the hustle and bustle of London.

Polly stared out of the window and yawned. It would have been nice to have chatted to Sam but he just turned away from her and scowled at the fast traffic whizzing along in the outside lane. Seeing his sour expression, Polly sighed irritably. Why couldn't Sam, just for once, be nice to their mum? It didn't take much to smile and it would make all the difference in the world to Mrs Styles who was sick with worry about him. Goodness knows, fumed Polly to herself, they all felt bad enough about leaving their London home but they had to do *something* after their dad had been made redundant.

Closing her blue eyes to the bright April sunshine, Polly's thoughts whizzed back to that awful day last October when her dad had walked into the kitchen where they were getting ready for supper. His usual cheerful face was grey and drawn.

'Dad!' she cried, frightened that he was ill. 'What's wrong?' Slumping into a chair, Ron Styles looked at his family and said, 'I've lost my job!'

Thunderstruck, they all stared back at him, their faces filled with total disbelief. Their mum was the first to speak.

'Ron, you're not serious?' she'd asked, hollow-voiced.

Mr Styles had nodded and buried his head in his hands.

'By Spring I'll be out of a job,' he'd muttered.

It was impossible! He'd been working at the same primary school in Streatham for ten years. He was deputy head teacher, in charge of sports and well on his way to a headship.

'Why *you*?' asked Mrs Styles, gob-smacked.

'Apart from the head I'm the eldest and I've been employed there the longest,' he explained. 'The school's staff quota has been cut by one – unfortunately that one is me.'

Lizzie Styles and Polly sat on either side of him, sharing his misery, but Sam disappeared upstairs to his room and soon the familiar sound of his Heavy Metal music was pounding through the ceiling. When it came to anything emotional Sam always hid his feelings, but as the weeks rolled by nobody, not even Sam, could hide away from the reality of their father's shattering news.

At first they all thought he'd get another job, in a nearby school. No such luck.

'It's cuts, cuts, cuts, all the way,' Mr Styles told them. 'I'm not the only one to lose my job under this education authority. We might have to consider a move,' he warned.

To start with nobody believed him. A brilliant teacher like Ron Styles was sure to get another deputy headship somewhere fairly close by. As the months passed and his job search extended out of London and into the southern counties, the penny slowly dropped. A big move was becoming a strong possibility. Nothing however, prepared them for a remote village in the wilds of Cambridgeshire.

'Cambridge!' Sam had snorted in disgust. 'Where's *that*?'

'Sam,' Ron Styles had patiently explained. 'I've answered an ad for a deputy headship in a place called Shelford. It sounds an interesting job.' He waited for Sam to say something but he didn't. 'I'm sorry, son, I have no choice but to go with the work.'

Sam had snarled something rude and stomped off upstairs.

The next day Ron Styles drove off for the interview and came back looking very pleased with himself.

'It's a lovely little village,' he said. 'The school's brilliant . . .' he paused, his eyes lighting up with excitement, then blurted out his news. 'I've got the job!'

Lizzie Styles went up like a rocket on Bonfire Night.

'It's only a year's contract,' he warned.

'I don't care!' she cried, her face creased with smiles of relief. 'It's a job, that's all that matters.'

'And, there's an added perk,' went on Mr Styles, mysteriously. 'There's a cottage close by which we can rent really cheaply for the next year.'

'Perfect,' sighed his wife.

'It's an old thatched cottage,' he continued. 'With a big garden and beautiful views across open meadows.'

Polly's heart had skipped a beat. Open meadows only meant one thing to her – horses! For years she'd longed to learn to ride but nothing had ever come of it, apart from the odd riding lesson on holiday in Cornwall. Maybe now, with a move to the country, it just might happen? Unfortunately they were so busy packing up their Streatham house and saying good-bye to their friends and family that there wasn't time to visit their new rented house in Shelford, but Polly carried her bright new hope all the way through the hectic weeks up to their departure.

The real shock of leaving only hit her when the removal men emptied her bedroom. Standing in the doorway, she could see the picture she'd scrawled behind her bed when she was three. The window gaped liked a bare hole now that her bright curtains were down and the room she'd loved so much echoed like an empty shell. Weeping, she ran out of the house and jumped into the back of her mum's car.

'Good-bye. Good-bye,' she whispered to the landmarks of her childhood. Suddenly the old familiar streets were gone as they headed east out of London.

When they got to Shelford it was just getting dark and the electricity they'd been expecting to be turned on was in fact turned off. When Mr Styles arrived with the removal van a quarter of an hour later, he burst out laughing to see his family standing outside their new home.

'Now I know what to call this place,' he said. 'Wit's End!'

Even with the light fading fast, Polly liked the pretty thatched cottage with the honeysuckle winding its way around the front porch, filling her nostrils with its pungent fragrance. From the tallest apple tree in their front garden a blackbird sang his heart out to the shining, new moon. Polly stood under the tree and smiled up at the bird.

'Hello,' she whispered. 'We're your new neighbours.'

As darkness fell they all set to work, unloading everything out of the van and dumping it anywhere they could in the house. As the moon rose it lit up the rooms so that at least they had some light to find their way around. By ten o'clock they were unpacked and exhausted.

'What wouldn't I give for a cup of tea!' gasped Lizzie Styles, perched uncomfortably on a packing case.

At that exact moment there was a knock on the door and there stood a large, smiling woman with a loaded tray in her hands.

'Excuse me, duck,' she said, walking in and carefully putting the tray down on the nearest packing case. 'I don't want to make a mess and drop this lot, do I?' When her hands were free she turned and beamed at them all. 'I'm Sue

Benton, from next door, and I was just saying to my husband Reg, I bet those folks from London will be needing a nice cup of tea and something to eat . . .' As she spoke she handed round steaming mugs of tea and big, thick ham and salad sandwiches. They were delicious. 'Now, in the morning, just you let me know when you're ready for a cuppa and I'll put the kettle on. The door's always open, so pop in whenever you fancy.' With another beam she was gone, like a smiling fairy godmother.

'What a lovely lady,' said Mrs Styles with a tired smile.

'Magic,' Dad agreed as he polished off his sandwich. 'Come on, let's go up to bed before we all fall asleep down here on the packing cases.' The removal men had taken their beds upstairs. Sam was in the large attic, Polly was in the front bedroom and her parents were in the back.

'You'll have to make do with sleeping bags,' Mum said. 'There's no way I can find duvets and bedding at this time of night.'

Saying good-night, Polly stepped into her new room and closed the door. The moon shone through the double latticed window, casting a pattern onto the sloping wooden floor and drenching her bed in silver light. She sniffed in the scents of the night. Outside, honeysuckle mixed with apple blossom, inside a spicy concoction of mothballs, beeswax and a hint of lavender. Quickly taking off her jeans and sweatshirt, Polly wriggled into her sleeping bag and closed her eyes. There were no curtains to draw across her window so she dozed off with the moon shining on her smiling face, dreaming of what tomorrow might bring . . .

Chapter Two

A Room with a View

The riotous birdsong of the dawn chorus and the sun streaming through her bedroom window woke Polly early the next morning. Looking around her new room, prettily decorated with old-fashioned wallpaper festooned with garlands of roses, Polly momentarily wondered where she was. Then she remembered – Wit's End, their new home! Jumping out of her sleeping bag she padded barefoot across the floor and stared out of her window. Blinking against the bright sun she rubbed her eyes . . . then rubbed them again!

Was she dreaming or had she died and gone to heaven?

There in front of her, across the street from their garden gate, was a rolling paddock, hazy with long-stemmed cow parsley and buttercups. Grazing peacefully in the soft morning mist were *ponies!* Polly pushed open her latticed window and leant out on the sill, her head brushing the honeysuckle that climbed up to their thatched roof. Staring like one bewitched she counted the peaceful ponies. A bay, a piebald, a silver grey, a palomino and a tubby Shetland. Suddenly the Shetland snorted and kicked up her back legs. The others lifted their heads and quickly moved out of the way as a woman, blonde hair flying out from underneath her riding hat, galloped across the paddock. Laughing at the indignant ponies, the rider collected in her stunning dark bay thoroughbred and headed for the cross-country course that wound its way over the open fields. Holding her breath, Polly watched the sixteen hands bay soar over everything he was put to. The woman sat deep in the saddle, almost one with the horse, going over the jumps with a speed and confidence that took Polly's breath away.

'Wowee!' she gasped as the rider disappeared out of sight and the ponies returned to their grazing, gently nuzzling their way through the buttercups.

For years and years Polly had adored ponies, but always from a distance. Riding lessons weren't the easiest thing to arrange in London and anyway they were expensive. To a large extent Polly had kept her passion under control. She'd always enjoyed reading pony books and she'd stuck several posters of beautiful ponies on the wall over her bed. Best of all were the family holidays in Cornwall where they always stayed on a farm just outside Penzance. The farmer's wife kept ponies for her own children and let Polly ride out with her every day. It was the highlight of her year. Unfortunately, Polly always returned to London life moody and irritable. It wasn't the rolling Cornish hills she missed but the ponies. Gazing out of her window at five of them was like a vision!

Her mother's voice calling her from downstairs reminded Polly that she was earth-bound.

'Polly – breakfast!'

Starving hungry but unable to tear her eyes from the paddock, Polly feasted on the ponies for five minutes longer then rushed downstairs, nearly falling head over heels in her excitement.

'Mum! Dad!' she yelled. 'There are ponies – right outside my window!'

Mr and Mrs Styles were delighted to see their daughter's radiant face.

'Well, I'm glad somebody's happy,' said her dad. 'Sam's really fed up.'

'I'll go and tell him breakfast's ready,' Polly volunteered.

When she opened Sam's door she knew from his breathing that he was awake but pretending to be asleep.

'Sam, Sam,' she said. 'Come on, get up.'

'Go away,' he growled like a bad-tempered lion.

'Oh, Sam, please cheer up,' she begged. 'It's such a beautiful day.' Her brother grunted, unimpressed.

'I don't like the country and I don't want to live in it.'

Polly sighed. If only Sam loved ponies he'd be as happy as she was. Unfortunately he loved London and Heavy Metal and the two went together in his mind.

'Please, give it a try,' she urged. 'It would make Mum and Dad so happy.' Frustrated by his silence she shook his sleeping bag. 'They're worried about you, Sam.'

'So, why did they leave Streatham?' he snapped.

Polly, who'd been through too many similar arguments with him before the move to Shelford, shrugged her shoulders.

'You know exactly why they left – they had no choice,' she poked him hard in the back. 'Stop lying here feeling sorry for yourself and come down for breakfast.' Sam didn't move so Polly went down without him, irritated by his selfishness.

It was impossible to stay cross with anybody for long on such a perfect spring morning. The kitchen door was open to the garden, bright with daffodils and tulips, and a swallow swooped in and out of their thatched roof, flashing its long dark tail feathers as it dipped and swerved in the pale blue sky.

Suddenly there was a thudding on the stairs and Sam appeared. Polly smiled as she poured out her crispies – something told her this move to the country was going to be the best thing that had ever happened to the Styles family.

There was so much unpacking, cleaning and tidying to do that Polly hardly had time to catch her breath. Hot and sweaty as she was, it was nice to see her bedroom take shape. She insisted on having her bed against the wall, facing the window.

'Won't the sun wake you up in the morning?' her mum asked.

'I jolly well hope so!' Polly answered with a happy smile. Her green and pink duvet looked fresh and bright against the old-fashioned wallpaper, and the polished sloping floor shone against a multi-coloured rug her mum had put down. There was a lovely cast iron fireplace with blue and white tiles, and into the open grate Polly put a vase containing buttercups and daisies. With the window open and her lace curtains fluttering in the breeze, the room looked like something out of a stylish magazine.

'Made for you,' said her dad, as he knocked nails into the wall for her mirror and pictures.

As soon as lunch was over Polly ran down the path and across the road. Standing on her tip-toes she could see over the hawthorn hedge into the paddock. The pretty chestnut pony was grazing close by and he looked up surprised when Polly tweaked her hand through the hawthorn blossom. Hoping that there might be a sweet in her outstretched hand, the chestnut neighed softly and ambled over. The next thing Polly felt was a warm mouth on her hand and a tongue licking her fingers.

'That tickles,' she cried.

'Belle, stop that at once,' said a voice so close behind Polly that she jumped sky-high.

'I'm sorry. I didn't mean to give you a fright,' Mrs Benton, their new neighbour, said with a loud laugh. 'I always pop over after lunch with a little treat for the ponies.'

Hearing her voice the ponies trotted across the field and pushed against the hedge.

'Aren't they gorgeous?' Polly said.

'Gorgeous, yes,' Mrs Benton agreed, then added with a knowing wink. 'And very, very greedy.'

As if to prove her point a pony's nose popped through the leaves and licked her arm.

'Hold on, hold on, I can't see you,' Mrs Benton called and quickly walked along the path until she came to a five-bar gate. 'That's better,' she said, reaching into her pinafore pockets and taking out a handful of red apples. 'Who's first?'

The five ponies pushed and jostled.

'Manners,' Mrs Benton said sharply. 'What will Polly think of you?'

To Polly's complete amazement the ponies stopped pushing.

'I always make them wait their turn,' Mrs Benton explained. 'Belle first,' she said, holding out an apple to the little chestnut who gently took it and quickly trotted off. 'Now Galaxy,' she continued, patting the gentle palomino who took a nibble then nervously backed off. 'Come on, finish it off,' Mrs Benton urged.

'You know them all so well,' Polly said, enviously.

'So would you if you visited them every day.'

Mrs Benton held out another apple to the stunning silver grey with a floating mane and tail.

'She's fabulous,' Polly sighed dreamily. 'What's her name?'

'Merlin,' said Mrs Benton. 'She's a real little lady.'

The fat Shetland pony came bumbling up, crossly pushing the others out of her way.

'Tara-boom-di-ay!' laughed Mrs Benton, giving her an apple. 'Tara for short and definitely the boss round here.'

The last pony came shyly up, a little bay with a delicate head and nervous eyes.

'Rosie,' said Mrs Benton. 'Always the shyest of the bunch.' The pony nibbled at the apple. 'You should see her jump, goes like a rocket.' When the ponies had finished their apples they jogged off into the long buttercups.

'Who do they all belong to?' Polly asked.

'The riding school,' Mrs Benton explained. 'That's it,' she added, pointing to a rambling Victorian house with a long drive. 'The stables and yard are just behind the house.'

'A riding school – in the village?' Polly gasped. 'I don't believe it.'

'You'd better,' Mrs Benton answered. 'Here comes the owner.' Polly turned at the sound of horse's hooves trotting along the road and saw the blonde woman she'd watched jumping the cross-country course earlier that morning. She was now riding a magnificent Irish Draught chestnut with a long golden mane.

'Morning Mrs Benton,' she called cheerfully.

'Morning Miss Reynolds. Had a nice ride?'

It was only when the woman turned and smiled that Polly saw she had a long scar running across her right cheek. Trotting smartly, she headed up the drive and into the stables.

'That's Miss Reynolds, Terry Reynolds.' Mrs Benton waited expectantly for some response from Polly. 'The ex three-day eventer,' she added. Polly looked totally blank. 'Sorry, lovie, I'd forgotten you weren't from round these parts,' Mrs Benton apologised. 'She's a famous rider, used to ride in all the big shows, even got through to the Olympics one year. She was quite a celebrity in those days. We had lots of famous people through here visiting her, even the Royal Family,' she added importantly. 'Then she took a terrible tumble at Burleigh Horse Trials five years ago and seriously damaged her back. People said she'd never walk again – well she has! She runs her own school nowadays and though she can't event herself she's the best teacher going. Run over and introduce yourself,' she suggested.

Polly stared at her, thunderstruck.

'Introduce myself?' she gasped. It would be

like walking up to the Queen of England and asking her home for tea! 'No . . .. not yet,' she answered nervously.

'You needn't be shy of Miss Reynolds,' Mrs Benton said as they wandered back home together. 'She has half the girls in the village working in her yard every weekend.'

Polly said goodbye to Mrs Benton and walked into the kitchen, her blue eyes as big as saucers.

'What's up with you, Pol?' her dad teased. 'You look like you've had a vision.'

'Oh, I have,' Polly sighed.

'What?' her mum asked, curiously.

'Ponies,' Polly murmured. 'Belle . . . Galaxy . . . Merlin . . . Tara . . . and Rosie.' Her parents looked at each other and smiled.

'Do you think there's something funny in the water round here?' her dad teased.

'No, Dad,' Polly answered. 'Everything's perfect, absolutely perfect!'

Chapter Three

Vida

Excited by the sight, sound and smell of so many ponies, Polly decided it was time to get an in-depth equine education. No way was she introducing herself to the dazzling Terry Reynolds until she knew exactly how to groom, tack up and ride. The pony books she'd read in the past only skimmed the surface; now she wanted to know *everything* the horse manuals could provide. Luckily it was still the Easter holidays, and though her mum and dad were keen for Polly to lend a hand with wall-papering and decorating, she managed to escape to the peace and quiet of Shelford library.

On her way there she passed the local recreation ground where lots of children gathered every day during the holidays. Polly particularly noticed a crowd of lively girls who stopped and nudged each other as she walked by. Obviously word had got round the village that a new family had moved in. Polly realised with a shock that ponies had so completely filled her mind she hadn't even thought about village life, starting school or even making new friends. She'd hardly given a moment's thought to her old friends back in Streatham. With a week to go to the start of term, she wondered what Shelford primary school would be like.

Once inside the library, with her face buried in a book on showjumping, school was the very last thing on her mind. Fascinated by the different jumps – spreads, gates, crossed poles, cavelletis, parallels and pyramids – Polly devoured each page of the book, imagining herself on a graceful little pony zooming over doubles, trebles and combinations, then winning the biggest rosette in the show! No sooner had she finished one book than she was on to the next. Feeding your pony, clipping, shoeing, feeding and grooming. By lunch-time Polly's head was whirling with horse-talk.

She walked back home with four library books tucked under her arm, and stopped at the paddock gate to say hello to all the ponies. Delighted to find a new one had joined the group, Polly patted a pretty dun with soft eyes and a kind expression.

'What's your name?' she asked.

To her surprise somebody answered.

'Cyder.'

Polly turned round and smiled at one of the village girls she'd seen earlier that morning on the recreation ground.

'Hello. I'm Vida,' said the girl. 'I heard you chatting to Cyder so I thought I'd chat to you.'

Polly beamed, instantly liking Vida, a tall, slim Indian girl with wonderful dark hair that hung in a thick plait all the way down her back.

'I'm Polly,' she said. 'How do you know the ponies?'

'I help out in Miss T.'s yard every Saturday,' Vida explained.

'Miss T.?' Polly asked.

'Terry Reynolds,' Vida said. 'We all call her Miss T.'

'You help *her*?'

'Quite a few of us do. We can't afford lessons every week, it gets expensive,' Vida added confidentially. 'So we muck out the stables and clean the yard on the Saturdays we don't ride.

It's great fun and best of all we can be near the ponies all day.'

Polly nodded her head in agreement.

'It sounds wonderful,' she sighed.

'You should give it a go,' Vida suggested. 'Why don't you come over with me this afternoon?'

'I'd love to,' Polly gasped. 'But I don't know very much. I've only ever ridden on holiday in Cornwall,' she admitted with a deep blush.

'None of us knew anything until we started working at the yard,' Vida admitted. 'But you soon find out when you roll your sleeves up and get stuck in.'

'Don't we need to make an appointment, or something like that . . . ?' Polly's voice tailed off as Vida burst out laughing.

'No!' she cried. 'We can wander over and see the ponies. Miss T. will probably be in the school, teaching, so we won't be under her feet. Where do you live?'

'Just across the road,' Polly said, pointing to their cottage.

'I'll call for you about two. Is that alright?'

Polly stared at her, stunned.

'Oh, yes!' she cried.

When Vida had gone Polly was left gazing at the ponies, her heart beating so fast she had to pause for breath.

'I'll be visiting you lot, *officially*, this afternoon,' she said.

The ponies pushed and jostled. They didn't care when or how she visited just as long as they got their mints and a cuddle.

'Sorry to keep you waiting,' she said, smiling at their eager, serious faces as she fumbled with the sweet wrappers. 'Here you are.' She held out the mints one at a time and the ponies moved forward, pushing each other out of the way. Polly hadn't quite mastered Mrs Benton's commanding style so it was a bit of a free for all until Tara bustled in, nipping and shoving, as if to say she was having no rowdy business in her field!

Her dad had been out to buy fish and chips for lunch but Polly was too excited to eat.

'Come on, love,' Mrs Styles urged. 'You'll need some energy if you're riding this afternoon.'

'I'm not riding,' she explained. 'Vida's just taking me over for a look round the yard.'

'Who's taking you?' Sam asked, looking up from his battered sausage and chips.

'Vida, a girl I met this morning.'

'What? Have you made friends already?' he asked in astonishment.

'She just came up and started talking to me when I was feeding the ponies.'

Her brother, who'd hardly set foot out of the house since they'd arrived in Shelford, looked blank.

'*What* ponies?' he puzzled.

Polly laughed at his baffled expression.

'Dope! The ponies opposite our front gate.' Sam shrugged.

'I dunno what you're on about,' he said.

'That's because you never go outside the front door,' Polly answered.

'Maybe you should go for a little walk, Sam,' Mrs Styles suggested. 'You might meet some boys and make friends.'

Sam scoffed dismissively.

'Village boys into Heavy Metal,' he scoffed. 'Do me a favour.'

Polly tactfully changed the subject before the meal ended badly. She was too happy to sit and listen to Sam moaning so she chatted about the library and the shops and the people she'd met in the High Street.

'You're a regular ambassador,' said her dad, proudly.

'A regular nosy-parker, if you ask me,' Sam muttered moodily.

Chapter Four

DIY

At two o'clock Polly was swinging on the garden gate, ready for action. She'd changed into her jeans, which looked too clean and pressed for stable wear, a sweatshirt with 'I love Palominos' written across the front and a pair of red wellies, just in case she did any mucking out. Glancing at herself in her bedroom mirror she grimaced.

'I don't look like any of those posh Pony Club girls in the books I've been reading,' she thought to herself. But who cared – she was going to have fun!

Vida arrived, wearing almost exactly the same sort of clothes as Polly, except for her footwear. She had on a pair of smart black jodphur boots. As they walked along the road to the yard Vida chatted about the village school.

'It's good,' she said. 'Very relaxed and easy going. Our headmaster's called Brian Glover, he's really funny, loves folk singing and Morris Dancing.' She laughed as she described their last school garden party. 'Mr Glover brought his band of Morris Men and we all joined in, shaking tambourines and whacking sticks. It was such a laugh!' Polly laughed too. Shelford school was beginning to sound very unusual.

'I hope I'll be in your class,' she said, shyly.

'How old are you?' Vida asked.

'Just turned ten.'

'You will,' she exclaimed. 'I'm ten next month and my best friend, Ella, who's away right now, is already ten. Great, we'll all be together.' Laughing like old friends they walked up the drive and into the yard.

'Here we are,' Vida announced then laughed at the sight of Polly's face. 'What's up?'

'It's *enormous!*' Polly gasped, her jaw hanging loose as she gazed around the yard in total astonishment. Compared to the small stables with a lean-to hay barn that Polly was used to,

Miss Reynold's set up was very grand. The yard was big and clean as a whistle, with a muck heap in the far corner that was so perfectly smooth and well-shaped it looked like it had been designer built. The stables ran in blocks of ten around the yard, with tack rooms and feed rooms at the end of each block. Horses' heads popped over the top of various doors at the sound of the girls' voices. One pale, pretty palomino whinnied shrilly.

'That's Fudge,' Vida said with a loving smile. 'My favourite.' She patted her bulging jeans pocket. 'He knows I never come empty handed.'

There was an enormous timbered barn where hay and straw were stored with a little thatched office next to it. Vida explained that this was Miss T.'s office.

'We call it her den and sneak in to see her photographs. She's got hundreds, in frames all around the wall. Badmington, Burleigh and the Olympics. She looked so young and beautiful.' Vida sighed wistfully. Suddenly Miss T. strode out of the office, her long blonde hair tied loosely back in a black velvet band. Wearing cream jodphurs and a soft blue shirt she looked stunning. Polly stared at her and gulped.

'Hi Vida,' she smiled warmly. 'Looking for a job?'

'Wouldn't mind,' Vida answered eagerly. 'By the way, this is Polly, she's just moved into the village and she's mad about horses.'

'Not another,' Miss T. answered with a laugh. 'Pleased to meet you Polly. Welcome to Shelford Riding School.'

Polly couldn't speak, she just smiled as if her face would split in half.

'The farrier's due at three and I'll be teaching in the school all afternoon,' Miss T. said to Vida. 'Could you hold Fudge, Belle and Tara for Mr Wilson?'

Vida beamed.

'I'd love to.'

'You'll have to get Belle and Tara from the paddock; Fudge is already in his box. Is that OK?'

Vida nodded.

'Fine. Polly will help me.'

'Good,' Miss T. answered briskly. 'See you both later.'

Polly stared after her hurrying figure, envious of her long legs, slim hips and strong back.

'She's so beautiful,' she murmured.

'Apart from the awful scar on her cheek. You must have seen it?' Vida asked.

'Yes, of course, but somehow it doesn't spoil her looks,' Polly said. 'How did she get it?'

'At Burleigh Horse Trials five years ago. She

ripped her cheek open when she took a fall at the water jump.' Vida shuddered. 'Can you imagine breaking your back and damaging your face all on the same day?'

'I'd rather not,' Polly admitted.

'Come on, we'd better get a move on before the farrier arrives.'

First they picked up the head collars from the sweet-smelling tack room where the ponies' and horses' names were written around the walls. Underneath each name was a brass hook for bridles and reins and a saddle rest. Polly could have spent hours inspecting the different bridles and saddles but Vida tugged at her arm.

'You can do that later,' she said. 'Here's the lunge line. It'll take ages to catch Tara.'

Polly looked at the long roll of thick canvas.

'What's this for?' she asked, puzzled.

'You'll find out in five minutes time,' Vida said with a laugh.

When they walked into the paddock Tara took one look at the head collars they were carrying and set off across the field like a rocket.

'Little demon,' Vida said. 'Let's get Belle first, she's always a lady.' Walking through the buttercups towards the chestnut Vida talked softly and held out her hand. Belle eagerly trotted towards her and nuzzled her palm, crunching happily on the two mints she found there. Without any fuss Vida was able to slip the head collar on, then tie her to the gate post by the lead rein.

'Now for Bossy Boots,' she said in a determined voice.

Tara 'Bossy Boots' was at the other end of the field looking very uncooperative.

'She's always difficult to catch when the new grass is coming up,' Vida explained. 'She thinks we're going to pen her.'

'Why would you pen her in now?' Polly asked, keen to learn as much as she could from Vida. 'She must be enjoying the spring grass after the long, wet winter?'

'Ponies get Laminitis. It's an acute inflammation of the feet and causes terrible pain. It can even kill them if they're allowed to eat too much grass. The only way to stop them eating is to either stable them during the day or keep them in a penned-off area. You have to be cruel to be kind with overweight ponies like Tara,' she said firmly. 'Now, you take hold of one end of the lunge line and I'll take the other then head for the corner where she's standing.'

When Tara saw the girls approaching with the line she snorted and galloped across the paddock.

'We've got to outsmart her,' Vida said. 'Stand as close to me as you can and we'll hide the line behind our backs.'

Polly did as she was told and they walked slowly towards Tara who watched them with a sharp beady eye. Vida nudged Polly as they closed in on the Shetland.

'Space out and get ready to run towards her with the line.'

As they separated, Tara caught sight of the lunge line and tried to run but the girls had cornered her, Polly on one side, Vida on the other, with the line between them, blocking her path. Snorting crossly Tara accepted her fate and let Vida slip the pink head collar over her neck.

'Come on, cheeky,' Vida said in a mock cross voice. 'Time to have new shoes on those pretty little feet.'

Leading Belle, Polly followed Vida and Tara to the stable block where Bob Wilson, the farrier, was already waiting for them.

'Who do you want first?' Vida asked.

'Tara,' said Bob with a knowing wink. 'It's important never to waste a lady's time.'

Polly watched fascinated as Bob set to work. First he trimmed Tara's tiny feet then fitted the new shoes, neatly tapping in the nails then filing the hoof around each shoe. Tara stood quiet as a mouse, leaning dreamily against Bob as he lifted each foot.

'She doesn't mind a bit,' Polly said to the blacksmith.

'She'd soon let me know if she did,' Mr Wilson said with a wry smile.

Polly laughed as Tara scratched the side of her face against the farrier's bottom.

'To the manner born is this one,' said the farrier, laughing too.

When Tara was finished, Vida held Belle while Polly led Tara back to the paddock. The little Shetland seemed to enjoy the crisp, clean sound her new shoes made and trotted briskly across the yard, her long black tail sweeping the ground behind her. Once in the paddock she neighed loudly at the other ponies as if to say, 'Hello! I'm back.'

'There you are,' Polly said, taking off her head collar. 'Go and show off your new shoes.'

To Polly's surprise Tara stood looking at her, then pawed the ground. Polly giggled at the cunning little pony.

'Are you trying to tell me I've forgotten something?' she teased. Tara pawed the ground again then shoved her nose against Polly's jeans pocket.

'Mints,' Polly said holding them out to Tara who solemnly crunched them then trotted off to join the other ponies.

Belle was nearly finished by the time Polly got back to the yard.

'Could you get Fudge out of his stable?' Vida asked.

Feeling rather nervous, Polly found Fudge's head collar then walked towards his stable. He watched her carefully, clearly wondering who she was.

'I'm new,' she explained as she opened his stable door.

Fudge seemed to find her polite explanation perfectly acceptable. He licked her hand, nudged her in the chest then blew on her hair as if to say, pleased to meet you! Polly patted him then slipped on his head collar and lead him out to Mr Wilson who was clearly fond of the gentle Palomino.

'Hello there, boy,' he said as he stroked his long golden mane. Fudge nuzzled him like an old friend. 'I first met Fudge ten years ago,' Mr Wilson explained. 'He was neglected, beaten, a sad bag of bones. I reported the chap who owned him to the RSPCA and they rescued him. When I told Miss Reynolds about him she phoned the animal shelter and asked if she could look after him. They agreed to a six month trial period and that was ten years ago!' he added with a smile. 'This place wouldn't be the same without old Fudgie here.'

Polly stared into the soft eyes of the pretty

Palomino and her heart ached. 'How could anybody neglect such a trusting little pony?' she sighed.

'A lot of people do. I see some terrible sights on my travels but I always make sure they're reported.' Patting Fudge's neck he smiled. 'You're happy now though, aren't you boy?'

Fudge pushed his head against the farrier's chest, as if to say, perfectly happy, thank you.

When all the ponies had been shod, the blacksmith drove off in his battered old Land Rover and Vida said,

'Let's put the kettle on.'

Polly laughed, thinking she was joking.

'What kettle?'

'Follow me,' Vida said, mysteriously.

At the end of the hay barn was a small room for the riders' equipment. The wall was lined with dozens of riding boots, riding hats, Barbours and rain coats. The only furniture was an old tin chest stuffed with pony magazines, a beat up sofa and a table on which there was a kettle, some mugs, jars of coffee and a tin of dried milk.

'This is where we all hang out on a wet Saturday morning,' Vida explained as she plugged in the kettle and produced tea bags from her jeans pocket. 'It gets a bit squashed about ten minutes before our lesson starts. Everybody's shoving, and grabbing their hats or pulling on their boots. It's a riot.'

'How many people have lessons?' Polly
asked.

'What, altogether?' Vida thought for a while.
'There are about thirty people here on
Saturday morning, maybe more. In our class
there are six, no more.' She poured boiling
water into their mugs and spooned in the
dried milk. 'Our lessons are brilliant,' she
enthused.

'Tell me what you do with Miss T.' Polly
asked.

'We always start on the flat; walk, trot,
canter, half circles and full circles. Stuff like
that.' Vida handed Polly her steaming mug of
tea and sat on the sofa as she talked. 'Then we
use the trotting poles, that's a real laugh. All
leaning forward with our bottoms up to get
our jumping positions right.' Polly was lost but
she smiled at Vida's vivid description. 'Then
onto the gridwork – small jumps with two
strides in between, gets us all warmed up and
bouncy, then – big time!' Vida's voice
quickened with excitement. 'A two to three
foot jumping course, with poles, a spread, a
gate, sometimes a double. Brilliant!' For all
her library research, the fine details of the
riding lesson were lost on Polly but she
loved hearing Vida talking and caught her
excitement. 'If there's enough time we end

with gymkhana games, they're the best fun of all—'

Their conversation was brought to a halt by the sudden appearence of a silver Volvo sweeping into the yard.

'Oh, no!' Vida groaned. 'Not Jessica "Snooty Pants" Pemberton.' As the Volvo eased to a halt a pretty girl about Polly's age, with long silver hair, pale, delicate skin and aloof blue eyes climbed out of the front seat. Dusting fluff off her immaculate white jodphurs and pink sweatshirt she looked around the yard as if she owned it. Polly gazed at her, stunned.

'Who is she?' she whispered to Vida.

'She's the girl with *everything*,' Vida explained. 'Her mum chauffeurs her about like royalty, *and* she owns Merlin, the perfect pony—'

'Merlin, the silver grey in the paddock?'

Vida nodded.

'The only pony I know who's colour coordinated to match his owner and the family Volvo.'

Polly giggled at Vida's remark.

'Merlin's at livery here. No such thing as DIY for the Pembertons.'

Vida gazed after Jessica and her elegant mother walking across the yard towards the paddock.

'Lucky girl,' Polly sighed.

'Never mind,' Vida cried, producing two squashed chocolate biscuits from her pocket. 'You don't have to be rich to have fun at Miss T.'s yard!'

Chapter Five

New Girl

With Vida to guide her through the early days, starting school at Shelford Primary was a breeze!

The first person Polly met was Ella, Vida's best friend who'd been away at her grandparents' house most of the Easter holidays. The two girls couldn't have looked more different – Vida was tall and on the thin side, Ella was small and chunky. Ella's hair was short, blonde and spiky and her eyes were an impish greeny-blue. Polly's first impression of Ella was that she was a bit of a tearaway and she was right too. Ella would do anything for a laugh. Everybody liked her, even their teacher, Ms Johnson, once she had her under control.

'Welcome to the workhouse,' Ella joked as Polly walked into their classroom.

Polly laughed. The workhouse was exactly what Ms Johnson's classroom wasn't. Big and airy with bright pictures and windows that opened wide onto fields, trees – and horses! From her place Polly could see acres of ripening wheat fields, with a bridle path running along the side, much used by Miss T.'s older riders. On her first morning just after assembly, Polly was settling down to some reading when she felt a sharp jab in her ribs.

'Look out of the window,' Ella hissed.

Polly followed the sound of clip-clopping hooves and saw a rider about fifty metres up the bridle path. It was a woman, swaying awkwardly on a big grey Polly had seen at livery in Miss T.'s yard.

'It's Galahad,' Vida whispered. 'Poor old boy, he's really not enjoying himself.'

'Would *you*?' Ella asked.

The girls watched mesmerised as the overweight lady rider lumbered into a clumsy trot, her wide bottom banging the saddle at all the wrong moments.

'Poor Galahad,' Ella whispered. 'If he survives that he'll survive anything!'

Fortunately the rider disappeared from sight and the girls turned their wavering attention back to their books, but not for long. Suddenly they heard a horse neighing and the heavy pounding of hooves.

'Oh, no! He's thrown her,' Vida gasped.

She was right. Galahad came cantering down the bridle path, sweating and agitated, with the big lady chasing after him, waving her riding whip. In a flash Ella was on her feet, yelling through the open window.

'Stop! Don't hit him!'

'Ella. Sit down!' Ms Johnson called.

Ella didn't hear, she was too busy telling the woman what to do.

'Get hold of his reins – slowly!' she called as the woman snatched clumsily at the flying reins. 'Don't frighten him or he'll run onto the road,' Ella warned.

Fighting back her panic the woman did as she was instructed. When she eventually got hold of the reins she slowly walked Galahad back down the bridle path to the yard.

'Phew . . .' Ella sighed, settling back into her seat. 'That was a close shave.'

'Thank you, Ella, for that lesson on horse control,' Ms Johnson said.

'We seem to have lost our reading period

and replaced it with something entirely new to the National Curriculum.'

'But Miss—' Ella started.

'Just *read!*' Ms Johnson said. 'At least until the bell goes.'

There were lots of other girls in the class, and some OK boys too, but Polly enjoyed Vida and Ella's company best of all. By the end of her first week she felt as if she'd been at Shelford Primary nearly a term – so did Ms Johnson.

'If you three girls would only put as much effort into your work as you do into drawing pictures of horses I'd be a happy woman,' she said to the three of them, after they'd drawn horses' heads on the front of every exercise book they could get their hands on.

Vida was the most diligent student, especially when it came to maths which she excelled at. Ella was half-hearted about everything except art. When Polly saw her drawings and paintings she was gob-smacked.

'They're brilliant!' she exclaimed as she went through Ella's art folder.

'I only started sketching when I started riding,' Ella told her. 'It sort of inspired me. First I drew horses and now I draw anything that moves.'

Her work was bold and bright, rather like Ella herself, with unexpected fine detail.

Examples of it hung in frames all along the school corridor.

'Wowee!' Polly gasped.

'Come on, you must be good at something too,' Ella said, generously.

'No,' Polly answered truthfully. 'Nothing so far, anyway.'

'Riding?' Ella suggested.

'Well, I can trot, canter, gallop and do all the obvious things. But I've never had any proper lessons and I've never jumped, well, not properly anyway.' She sighed wistfully. 'That's what I want to do most in the world.'

'Then you should have riding lessons,' Ella suggested.

Polly shook her head.

'Tricky,' she said and left it at that.

With her dad teaching in the same school she didn't want to go into any details on the family's financial position. She was sure her parents could manage a riding lesson once in a while but on a regular, weekly basis, no way. Polly knew her mum was especially worried about money and the last thing she needed right now was another expense. Vida saw the anxious look in Polly's eyes and immediately said,

'Just come along to the yard and help on Saturdays. That's what we always do, isn't it Ella?'

Ella nodded enthusiastically.

'It's the best laugh of the week – and we're with horses. What could be better?'

'Nothing,' Polly answered. 'Nothing at all.'

The following Saturday Polly waited for Vida and Ella at the top of Miss T.'s drive.

'Just go in, we'll find you,' Ella had said airily but Polly felt too shy to wander in on her own.

As she waited, she curiously watched other girls and boys arriving. Some were on bikes, some walked but most rolled up in cars. Several cars were held up beside Polly, waiting for a van to back down the drive. Staring idly into the back seat of the nearest car Polly got a shock to see Jessica Pemberton staring frostily back at her. Jessica had a peevish, irritated look on her pale pretty face which puzzled Polly. Was she impatient to be kept waiting or was she cross that somebody had the nerve to look into *her* car? Luckily Vida and Ella arrived and waving to Polly they dodged the parked cars and ran down the drive together.

It was Vida's and Ella's week to ride so Polly watched their lesson at nine o'clock in the outdoor school. Vida was on Fudge, Ella on Belle, a boy called Toby rode Galaxy, two other girls rode Cyder and Rosie and Jessica Pemberton queened it over them all on her breathtaking Merlin. As Polly perched on the fence she was filled with envy. Even if she managed to swing the odd lesson now and again it would take ages before she would be up to the standard of Vida and Ella. As they circled the school, warming up, Polly was immediately impressed by Jessica Pemberton's style.

'She has a private lesson every week with Miss T.,' Ella told her as she tacked up Belle. 'You'd think that would be enough for anybody but not Jessica Pemberton. She has to join us on Saturdays,' she pulled down her mouth in a grimace. 'I swear she only does it to make us all feel stupid!'

'No, it's not,' Vida interrupted Ella's tirade with a laugh. 'She's getting herself in shape for the summer Pony Club events.'

Ella stared at her friend, horrified.

'You haven't been talking to *Jessica Pemberton*?' she gasped.

'No, I heard Mrs Pemberton arranging it with Miss T.,' Vida explained.

'Well, I just wish she hadn't picked *our* class to shape up in,' Ella grumbled on. 'She's so good she puts me off!'

Polly laughed at Ella's furious expression but as she watched the lesson she began to see what Ella was talking about. Jessica Pemberton was very good, as was the boy, Toby. The other four riders, Vida and Ella included, were all roughly at the same stage. It was Miss T.'s skills as a teacher that brought the group together. She watched each pupil with an eagle eye, not letting any of them get away with a thing, whatever their level. If somebody was sitting badly or handling their mount carelessly she was onto them in a flash.

'Come along, Toby, you couch potato!' she yelled. 'You're out of balance and dreaming. Straighten up, and keep those elbows in, they look like knitting needles from where I'm standing.'

Toby took her comments in good humour, quickly correcting his position, concentrating more on the lesson than the girl behind him. Polly was impressed by Miss T. She was on the ball but she never bored her students, she just kept them moving, thinking, working for a good, solid hour.

They started on the flat as Vida had told Polly, walking, trotting and cantering in half circles and then full circles. After a good warm-up they moved onto the trotting poles which each rider took at a brisk trot, lifting their seats into the correct jumping positions and using their knees to maintain a good balance. Ella, of course, fooled around, sticking out her bottom like an indignant duck which reduced the class, apart from Jessica Pemberton, to screaming giggles.

'Thank you for that performance, Ella,' Miss T. called, obviously amused. 'Now let's see you do it properly this time.'

Down went Ella's bottom as she took the poles again. Polly was impressed by her balance and strength. She was a tough little rider, quite different from Vida whose style was gracefully elegant rather than punchy. As the class moved on to the gridwork Polly felt her body instinctively move in rhythm with the ponies. The jumps were small with two strides in between and Polly could feel the pace and timing.

'Go! Go!' she heard herself saying out loud as some of the riders hesitated at the jumps.

Miss T. stared across at her.

'You've got it right,' she said with a smile.

Polly shrugged, embarrassed.

'It's easy when you're sitting on a fence,' she said, jokingly.

When the class moved onto the small jumping course Polly stuck a toffee in her mouth, determined not to open it again until the lesson was over. There were about six jumps in all and the minute Vida, who happened to be the first rider, headed for the first spread, the crossed poles, Polly's pulse was racing. Her brain whizzed, her senses fused and she knew – *absolutely knew* – what to do. She held on to the gate post and pressed her thighs and knees tight into the wooden planks. She felt her body sway forwards, anticipating the height and fall of the jump as Vida took it. It was so exhilarating, so breathtakingly exciting that Polly's body began to shake as Vida completed the course.

'Clear round,' Miss T. called out. 'Well done Vida. Jessica, you next.'

Jessica Pemberton was stunning, and so was Merlin. Tossing his pretty silver mane he approached the first jump, striding perfectly to take-off. Jessica shortened her reins and sat well forward and Merlin zoomed over the cross-poles, moving quickly onto the spread.

'More speed this time,' Miss T. instructed.

Jessica put her leg on but kept her stride, setting Merlin perfectly at the spread, the gate and the double. The whole round seemed superb to Polly but Miss T. had a few comments as Jessica finished.

'A softer hand and leg next time,' she said.

As Jessica nodded and smiled at Miss T. Polly was surprised at how nice her face looked when she relaxed.

Next came Ella who was so excited she brought the cross poles down immediately.

'A bit less gusto and more deliberation. Sit still, Ella,' Miss T. said, calming Belle who was spooked by the falling poles.

'I'm sorry,' Ella gasped.

'You got Belle on the wrong leg,' Miss T. pointed out. 'One more try please.'

Ella nervously took the jump again and cleared it awkwardly but then she lost her bottle at the final gate which she clipped as she flew over.

'You must collect your pony and talk to her so that you're communicating with all your aids, Ella. Watch her ears and look over the jumps, not into them.' Miss T. patted Belle as Ella glumly listened. 'Better luck next time.'

The hour flew by and the next class started to gather for their lesson.

As one group left and the other filed in Miss T. turned to Polly and asked, 'Did you enjoy that?'

Polly nodded.

'Yes, I loved it.'

'I thought so. You were riding that fence like an old pro.'

Polly blushed.

'I got completely carried away,' she admitted.

'It's even more exciting on the real thing,' Miss T. added with a warm smile.

Polly hurried away as the next class started their warm-up exercises.

She found Ella and Vida untacking their ponies in the yard.

'Poor Belle, I gave her such a fright when I brought those wretched poles down,' Ella fretted.

'She's had harder knocks than that,' Toby called from inside Galaxy's stable.

'That's not the point,' Ella said. 'I've never frightened her before. Now she won't trust me.'

Near to tears, Ella buried her face into Belle's soft mane.

'Looking at the pair of you I'd say you were more upset than Belle,' Vida said. 'Come on, give her a drink of water, she must be thirsty.' Ella led Belle into her stable and gave her a drink of water and a hay net to nibble.

'There you are,' she whispered to her favourite pony. 'Have a snack before your next lesson.'

'What, another lesson after this?' Polly asked, astonished.

'She'll be working all morning,' Ella explained.

'It's a hard life,' Polly said.

'Weekends are hard,' Ella agreed. 'Weekdays are fairly quiet, except in the school holidays of course.'

Jessica Pemberton, who'd excluded herself from the group, walked by, leading Merlin back to the paddock.

'Lucky old Merlin,' Ella muttered. 'One hour

of work then it's back to the field.'

'Lucky old Jessica,' Toby added, leaning over Galaxy's stable door and staring enviously at Merlin's perfect proportions.

'I don't know' Polly mused. 'She doesn't look like a girl who's happy.'

She stopped short when she saw them all staring at her, thunderstruck.

'Not very happy – come on!' Toby scoffed.

'She's totally sorted,' Ella added.

'Maybe,' Polly said, but wondered why a girl who had everything should look so sad a lot of the time.

Chapter Six

Fat, Funny, Fickle Ponies!

Polly, Vida and Ella spent the day helping out around the yard. The rest of the morning was busy, helping the young riders tack up, then leading them across the yard to the school where on the hour, every hour, the classes changed over. At lunch time Miss T. stopped for a quick sandwich and a coffee in her office, before she started on the afternoon classes which were entirely for adult riders.

'At least it gives the ponies a rest,' Vida said as they led Belle, Galaxy and Rosie back to the paddock. Tara was waiting for them by the gate, neighing excitedly at their return.

'Alright, mother hen,' Ella teased as Tara nuzzled each of the ponies. 'Honestly, you'd think they'd been away for a month.'

The ponies rolled in the long buttercups, scratching their backs in an ecstacy of freedom. When they'd rolled to their hearts' content they stood up, had a good shake and got down to the serious business of eating!

'We can have a rest too,' Vida said, checking her watch. 'Half an hour for lunch before we start tacking up the horses for the next class.'

They hurried over to the boot room, as Ella called it, where at least half a dozen other helpers were sprawled all over the battered sofa, or on the floor, eating and sharing out their sandwiches and crisps. They ranged in age from about nine to fifteen, the two eldest being Vanessa and Tanya who both had mad crushes on Tom, Miss T.'s handsome young groom.

'Tell you what,' Tanya said, biting her banana. 'Tom was really cut up when Joshua was sold last week.' She paused dramatically. 'I went in to muck out Joshua's stable and found Tom wiping tears from his eyes.' She drank deeply from her Coke. 'Imagine a man crying?'

'I often cry,' Toby admitted cheerfully. 'Especially when Tara treads on my toe!'

Suddenly Tom the groom walked into the barn and put an end to the interesting discussion.

'Isn't he gorgeous?' Vanessa sighed and rushed off, giggling and blushing, to offer her assistance to the handsome groom.

'YUK!' Ella snorted, completely echoing Polly's feelings. They fell into a heated discussion about the best pony breeds and completely forgot the time until they heard Miss T. calling,

'It's nearly two o'clock.'

In a flash they were on their feet and hurrying across the yard. Most of the horses that were out in the fields had been brought into their stables, ready for tacking up.

'Polly, help Toby will you?' Miss T. called.

Polly nodded and quickly followed Toby to the block of stables at the opposite end of the yard. She would have preferred to have stayed with Vida and Ella, but they'd been sent off to help Vanessa and Tanya. Self-conscious to start with, she soon forgot her nerves as Toby handed her a set of tack and led her into Jupiter's stable.

'He's h-u-g-e!' she gasped, overawed by the sixteen hands dark bay.

'Soft as a lamb, aren't you Jupiter?' Toby said, confidently brushing Jupiter's silky mane from out of his eyes. Jupiter nudged Toby who fed him a mint before he started tacking up. 'Why don't you go next door and introduce yourself to Misty Dell. She's pawing the ground; that means she wants attention. I'll be with you in a minute.'

Misty Dell was curiously peering over her door, keen to get to know Polly. Smaller than Jupiter, about fifteen hands, she was a blue roan with a delicate face and alert eyes.

'Hi, there,' Polly said and walking into her stable she carefully tacked Misty up, taking extra care to get the straps and girths just right. When she glanced up she was surprised to find Miss T. standing watching her.

'Good,' she said, checking the bridle and girth as Polly walked Misty Dell out. 'I always keep a bit of a close eye on my new girls to start with. Well done.'

Polly smiled, pleased to have passed her first test, then ran off and joined the other girls mucking out the pony block.

By the time five o'clock came Polly was exhausted. She'd mucked out and hosed down five stables, straightened the muck heap and cleaned and polished three saddles and bridles – but she didn't want to go home.

'I've had it,' Ella said, yawning loudly.

'Me too,' Vida added. 'Let's get our things together.'

'Can't we stay a bit longer?' Polly begged.

'We could,' Ella said. 'But we might just get locked in for the night.'

Polly smiled.

'I wouldn't mind.'

'I would – I'm starving,' Vida cried.

Reluctantly Polly left the yard, waving goodbye to Miss T.

'Thank you,' she called. 'See you next week.'

Polly's heart sank like a brick. Next week seemed an eternity away. She had to see the ponies and the horses before then!

It was Polly's desire to see the ponies every day that led to her calling into the yard on her way back from school. At first she was shy and stayed out of Miss T.'s way, but then she realised that Miss T. was often relieved to see her.

'Oh, Polly. I'm glad you're here. Could you just finish filling the water buckets while I get the phone?'

Sometimes Polly would pop in for five minutes and stay two hours. Mixing the feeds, helping with the grooming, waiting for the vet, holding ponies for the farrier, mucking out! It was all wonderful.

One Monday afternoon Polly dropped by and Miss T. asked her to tack up Cyder for a private lesson. Polly brought the dun out of the paddock where she was being pestered by flies and gently cleaned her pretty face, especially around the eyes where she'd been badly bitten. She groomed Cyder, first with the dandy brush and then the body brush, and picked out her feet before tacking her up. When she was finished Cyder looked very handsome and pawed the ground, impatient to be off. Suddenly Miss T. came out of her office.

'They've just phoned to cancel the private lesson.' She scowled irritably. 'It makes me so cross when people cancel. The ponies get so frustrated.' She stopped and looked at Polly with a smile on her lips. 'Why don't you ride Cyder?' she asked.

'Me!' Polly squeaked. 'I haven't got any money, Miss T.'

'I don't want any money,' Miss T. answered dismissively. 'The lesson can be a thank you for all the hard work you've done. Get a hat and mount up, I'll meet you over in the school.'

Her heart racing with excitement, Polly tore across the yard to the boot room, grabbed a hat, pulled it on then ran back to Cyder who looked at her as if to say,

'I wasn't expecting *you!*'

Polly mounted and trotted briskly towards the school where Miss T. was waiting for her. Taking deep breaths she forced herself to stay calm and sensible.

'Make the most of it,' she muttered to herself. 'You won't get many free lessons in your life.'

Miss T. began the lesson with nice, slow trotting.

'What diagonal are you on?' she suddenly asked.

Knowing a diagonal was rising on the leg nearest the fence Polly could confidently answer,

'My left.'

'Good. Now change diagonal.'

Instead of taking the change slowly, Polly started kicking and flailing her arms about.

'For goodness sake,' Miss T. called out. 'You're not taking the poor horse to market, stop kicking her like that.' Miss T. was sensitive enough to see Polly's embarrassed expression. 'Don't worry about it, Polly, talking to ponies is a subtle language. You have to learn to communicate through your hands, your body and speech. It doesn't come overnight,' she added with a knowing laugh. 'Believe me.'

Soothed by her advice Polly started listening rather than reacting. Taking her time, waiting for Cyder's ears to prick up so that she knew she had her complete and undivided attention, Polly listened to Miss T. and carefully followed her instructions.

'Put your right foot just behind her girth

and just touch her flank with your heel. No jabbing! Good. Now sit for two beats. Excellent. Now rise when her inside leg goes forward.'

Polly rose on the movement.

'Excellent, Polly. Now bring your pony down to a walk and change directions, this time cutting the diagonal across the school. Knees in, heels down, keep your bottom heavy in the saddle.'

She watched Polly like a hawk, impressed by her ability to translate instructions into action. After twenty minutes of solid flatwork Polly felt like she was part of Cyder, an extension of her back and muscles.

'Make that straight line between the shoulders, the hips and the heel, don't jiggle or twitch. Keep it straight and clean.'

Polly adjusted her position, instinctively feeling for the line down the length of her body.

'Excellent!' Miss T. cried. 'Remember it.'

Polly nodded. Now she'd found it, how could she forget. It was the most comfortable position she'd ever had on a pony, as natural as breathing. After half an hour Miss T. brought Polly to a halt saying, 'Riding is a subtle business and requires the subtle art of communicating with your mount. The aids you've just learnt will tell your pony what to do, without the whole world knowing it too. You don't need signposts, like a kicking leg, to tell us that you're moving your pony on. The right touch on her flank is much neater and very effective. Hands are important too and so is the voice.' Miss T. smiled fondly as she tickled Cyder's ears. 'These are intelligent, sensitive animals.' Cyder chomped thoughtfully, as if to say, you're telling me! 'Talk to them, tell them what you're going to do – walk, trot, stop etc. Now – your hands.' Miss T. precisely rearranged Polly's hands. 'They're delicate instruments so don't fiddle and faff about with them. Keep them down and soft.'

In that glorious hour alone with Miss T. Polly learnt so many, many things. Skills the books could never give her, an intelligent awareness of the complexities of horses and their understanding. By the end of the lesson she was going perfectly, her brain completely synchronised with her body.

'Well done, that was very good, Polly,' Miss T. said as they walked back to the yard.

'I loved it,' Polly enthused, red with pleasure and excitement. 'Thank you so much.'

'A pleasure,' Miss T. answered, quickly adding, 'you have a natural seat, Polly, and learn quickly. It might be a good idea for you to have the odd lesson now and again.'

Polly gulped with delight.

'I'll try,' she answered, wondering how she'd manage it.

As she walked Cyder back to the paddock she suddenly knew exactly how she'd do it.

Chapter Seven

Miss T.

Polly ran out of the stables, down the High
Street to the newsagent's where she scoured
the window looking for the advertisement
she'd seen a few days earlier. Letting out a big
sigh of relief she spotted it and read it out loud
to remind herself.

'Wanted – reliable girl or boy to help with
garden.
£2 an hour, 2 hours a week. Phone, 62462'.

Luckily the number was easy to remember and

Polly ran home repeating it all the way. The moment she was in the house Polly phoned and an old lady answered, a bit on the deaf side.

'Hello, I'm Polly Styles. I live in Shelford and saw your advert in the newsagent's. Is the gardening job taken?'

There was a long pause.

'What?' the old woman asked, vaguely. This time Polly spoke in a much louder voice.

'The job you advertised in the newsagent's window.'

'Oh, that! Yes. I'm looking for somebody reliable, you know,' the old lady added. 'I've a big garden and I can't manage it on my own. How old are you?' she asked, hardly stopping for breath.

'Nearly eleven,' Polly answered, not wanting to lie but certainly wanting to make the most of her age.

There was another pause, then the woman said,

'Come tomorrow and bring your parents. You can never be too sure these days.'

'Where do you live?' Polly asked before the old lady put the phone down on her.

'The Grange – I'm Mrs Bevan.' This time the phone went down with a definite click.

Polly's parents weren't at all pleased at her plan to get a job.

'What about your school work?' her dad asked.

'It's only *two* hours a week,' she reasoned.

'Who is this Mrs Bevan?' her mum said.

Polly shrugged.

'I don't know but you'll find out tomorrow – she wants to meet you too.'

Before her parents could ask another question Polly moved on to the serious business.

'I want to do the job so that I can pay towards riding lessons,' she blurted out.

'Riding lessons!' her dad exclaimed. 'Aren't they a bit expensive?'

Before they could bombard her with questions Polly quickly continued.

'Yes, I suppose they are, if you ride weekly, but I'm not talking about that,' she added. 'Once a fortnight would be fine with me – and I'll pay most of the cost with my gardening money.'

'If you get the gardening job,' her dad added realistically.

'Ron!' her mum scolded. 'Polly's put a lot of thought and effort into this plan, don't put her down like that.'

Mr Styles smiled gently.

'Sorry, love. Go on.'

'Well, I was wondering if you could help me out a bit?'

Her parents stared at her. Polly gulped hard.

'You see, eight pounds won't quite cover the full hour.'

Mrs Styles gave her daughter a hug.

'Of course we'll help you out, love. Won't we Ron?'

Mr Styles nodded in agreement.

'I just don't want you tiring yourself out, gardening and riding.'

'Dad!' Polly cried. 'Riding's fun. It's not work.'

'And gardening?' her dad teased.

'I don't know a thing about it,' Polly admitted, laughing. 'But if it means riding lessons, I'll sprout green fingers overnight.'

The first question Mrs Bevan asked was,

'Have you done any gardening?'

Vividly recalling their pocket handkerchief garden in Streatham, Mrs Styles and Polly looked at each other and tried not to smile.

'A little,' Mrs Styles answered truthfully. 'But she's quite capable, I can promise you that.'

'And I'm very reliable,' Polly chipped in, remembering the phrasing of the ad in the newsagent's window.

Mrs Bevan stared at her as if she were a dodgy piece of new garden equipment.

'I'll give you a go,' she decided. 'As long as I have your mother's consent.'

Mrs Styles nodded her agreement.

'Two pounds an hour, that's four pounds a week for weeding and watering, to start with,' Mrs Bevan said.

Polly smiled, bright-eyed with excitement.

'Er, excuse me, Mrs Bevan,' Mrs Styles interrupted. 'I wonder if Polly might be paid on a fortnightly basis? She'll need the money every two weeks for her riding lesson, you see.'

'Suits me,' Mrs Bevan said – and the deal was done.

Polly did two hours the next day and another two at the end of the week, making only a few mistakes. In her enthusiasm, she pulled up Mrs Bevan's geranium seedlings whilst weeding the garden, and over-watered the roses. After a smart ticking off, Mrs Bevan got down on her knees and showed Polly the difference between chickweed and new seedlings, then took her into her old-fashioned kitchen where she gave her strawberry milkshake and a slice of home-made chocolate fudge cake. Polly smiled as she bit into the rich icing on the cake. She had a feeling that Mrs Bevan's bark was a lot worse than her bite.

After her two hours gardening Polly ran down the High Street to Miss T.'s yard to see the ponies she'd been dreaming about all day. First she said hello to the horses, all at livery, apart from Miss T.'s magnificent sixteen hands eventer, Pasadoble. Running a hand along his strong neck Polly moved on to pretty Misty Dell in the next stable. When she'd greeted all the horses Polly headed for the paddock where Cyder instantly lifted her head and neighed. Tara rushed to the gate as Polly opened it, keen to be first, quickly followed by Belle, Galaxy, Rosie and Fudge. Nudging and snuffling, they said their hellos then wandered off to graze in the sunshine. Smiling to herself Polly watched them go.

'I wonder which of you I'll be riding in a fortnight?' she said out loud.

Little did she know that as she spoke fate was taking an unexpected hand in things . . .

Chapter Eight

Surprises

Polly left the paddock and popped into Miss T.'s office.

'Any jobs want doing?' she asked, as usual. 'Oh, sorry,' she mumbled when she saw Miss T. was on the phone.

She waited outside where she could still hear some of Miss T.'s conversation.

'If she's a show pony why are they selling her on?' There was a pause and then Miss T. said, 'I'll drive over and take a look.' When Polly heard the phone go click she popped her head round the door.

'Any jobs, Miss T.?' she asked cheerfully.

'Yes, come with me,' Miss T. answered, picking up the keys of her old jeep.

Thinking they were going to get some feed Polly climbed in beside her and they set off along the country lanes for Whittlesford.

'I'm going to look at a pony that's just about to go to auction. She's a show pony gone wrong. We'll check her out.'

Polly's face lit up with excitement. Feeling very important she sat beside Miss T. as they drove the five miles to the private yard in Whittlesford. When they got there Bob Wilson, the farrier, was waiting for Miss T.

'The pony's called Moon Dancer, she's in the stable and I warn you she's a nervous wreck. I think she's been knocked about by one of the kids here,' his voice dropped to a confidential whisper. 'The owner's got a couple of maniac sons who think ponies are for beating up. The good news is Dancer's got potential and she's going dirt cheap.'

While Miss T. introduced herself to the owner, Polly wandered over to the stables and curiously peered into the gloom. She stopped dead. Staring at her from the dark interior of the stable was a twelve two, silver grey, Welsh Section A, with a flowing tail and mane. The sun slanting through the door fired her coat to a shimmering silver glow and lit up a face that was so soft and vulnerable it made Polly's heart ache.

'Hello. Did anybody ever tell you you're perfect?'

The pony stared at her thoughtfully. Polly held her gaze and smiled.

'Come on,' she said.

Suddenly the pony's ears went down and she backed nervously into the far corner of her stable.

'Here we are,' boomed the woman who owned her. 'Moon Dancer. Nice looking but no good for my boys. They need something they can really get stuck into. This one's all nerves and tension.'

Miss T. led the pony into the yard and Polly held her on the lead rope. Dancer didn't like the attention or the handling, but Polly managed to calm her, softly whispering her name as she fondled her mane.

'Shshsh, Dancer. You're fine.'

She was so intent on the pony that she didn't hear a word of the business deal going on around her. She loved the smell of Dancer, the silky bright delicacy of her coat, her neat feet and fine-boned legs, the sweep of her neck and curve of her flanks.

'You're just perfect,' she whispered.

'Could you put her back in the stable?' Miss T. asked, breaking into Polly's reverie.

Polly reluctantly led Dancer back into the stable where she nuzzled Polly's hand with her soft, warm mouth.

'I don't want to leave you,' Polly murmured.

At the sound of Miss T.'s jeep starting up she hurried across the yard. With a last, longing glance at Dancer she sighed as they drove away.

'What will happen to her?' she asked anxiously.

'I've just bought her. They're driving her over tonight.'

'Bought her!' Polly cried and jumped up so high she banged her head on the roof of the jeep. 'That's wonderful.'

Miss T. smiled to herself as she drove down the leafy lanes.

'I have a feeling that little pony is going to be a star,' she said, thoughtfully.

'She's perfect,' Polly breathed.

'She liked you,' Miss T. added.

Polly blushed with pleasure.

'You can ride her tomorrow.'

Polly shook her head, hiding her disappointment.

'No, I'm riding *next* week, after I've been paid by Mrs Bevan.'

'No you're not,' Miss T. answered with an impish grin. 'Your parents have booked you in for a lesson tomorrow.'

Polly's jaw dropped and her mouth hung open.

'I don't believe it!'

Miss T. drove up outside Polly's front garden.

'Go and check for yourself,' she said. 'Then get some sleep. Dancer will want you bright-eyed and bushy-tailed tomorrow morning.'

Polly rushed into the kitchen.

'Am *I really* having a riding lesson tomorrow?' she gasped.

Her parents smiled at each other and nodded.

'Good news travels fast,' her dad said.

Polly hugged him tight.

'Thank you, oh, thank you!' she cried, hugging her mum too.

'We thought you deserved it,' Mrs Styles explained. 'You've gone to such a lot of bother to sort out riding lessons and not trouble us for extra cash.'

'We do appreciate your efforts,' Mr Styles said. 'So we thought we'd treat you.'

'It's brilliant,' Polly said, beaming fit to burst. 'And you'll never guess . . .' she paused dramatically.

'Well, go on,' her dad teased. 'The suspense is killing me.'

'I'm going to ride Moon Dancer!'

Her parents looked blank.

'The new show pony Miss T.'s just bought. She said I can try her out tomorrow. Honestly, I don't think I'll sleep a wink tonight.'

Polly couldn't have been more wrong. The minute her head touched the pillow she was sound asleep, dreaming of gymkhanas and ponies with flying silver manes and tails.

Vida and Ella couldn't believe their ears when Polly announced she was having a lesson the next morning.

'But, but, but . . . ?' Ella mumbled.

'It's a surprise from my parents,' Polly explained.

It was an even bigger surprise when she walked out of the stable leading Dancer.

'Wow!' Vida gasped. 'She's lovely.'

'Where did she come from?' Ella drooled, running her hands along Dancer's shimmering flanks.

'Miss T. bought her yesterday and,' Polly breathlessly added, 'I'm riding her!'

'Lucky you,' Vida said, rubbing Dancer's soft pink nose.

'Give me a leg up,' Polly said as the other riders trotted out of the yard. 'Wish me luck!'

As Polly trotted into the school she was filled with an odd confidence.

'We can help each other,' she whispered to

Dancer. 'You can teach me everything I need to know and I can look after you.'

Dancer tossed her delicate head, as if to say, it's a deal!

The lesson started on the flat then moved onto gridwork and trotting poles. The first half hour progressed calmly, though Dancer did have a tendency to shy at the other riders if they passed by too close to her. Once or twice she stopped short, as if she were suddenly afraid she'd done something wrong. Miss T. watched with an eagle eye, ready to step in and help, but Polly seemed to have the pony under control. Gently talking her through the lesson, she calmed her with a pat and moved her on with gentle pressure on her flanks. Dancer responded immediately to her gentleness and Polly could see her thinking things through as her ears moved back and forth, listening to her. All went well until the jumping course was set up, and Dancer started freaking out. She seemed to hate the noise and the activity around her and when she saw the gaudy red and white spread she backed off as if she'd seen a ghost. Miss T. was immediately beside Polly.

'Don't push her,' she warned Polly. 'Move her onto the planks, see how she responds to them.'

Polly did as instructed and though Dancer

didn't back off she certainly wasn't in the mood for going over. When Toby came up unexpectedly close behind them Dancer panicked. Her ears went down and she seemed terrified of being hit from behind.

'Shshh,' Polly soothed, turning her away from the jump and Toby's over-zealous mount.

'Take her into the paddock and calm her down,' Miss T. called. 'She's done well so far, let's leave it at that.'

As Polly trotted Dancer out of the school she saw Jessica Pemberton smirk, as if to say, what can you expect from a novice and a second rate hack?

Once in the paddock Dancer relaxed and sniffed the sweet air. She tossed her flowing mane and moved into a brisk, comfortable trot.

'So, little lady, you don't like jumping?' Polly said. 'Did somebody give you a fright?' Dancer's ears were pricked, she was listening to every word Polly spoke. 'Well, you mustn't worry about things any more.'

Dancer relaxed underneath her and opened out into a smooth canter. Setting a lovely stride Polly could feel the power pulsing through her. Suddenly they were heading out towards the cross-country course. As one of the jumps loomed into view Polly felt an instant change in Dancer's rhythm.

'She's going to jump!' Polly thought in total disbelief. 'Cool it,' she called to Dancer. 'You're not ready for this – neither am I!' she added but Dancer had other plans. On an extended canter she was going for the jump. Polly could have pulled her back but something told her not to – Dancer was doing this to prove something to her. Gulping, she collected Dancer in and looked straight through her ears, past the jump, rather than into it. When she felt Dancer's front legs lift she moved all her weight forward and rose with her, soaring up and over what looked like an enormous drop. As Dancer touched down Polly sank gratefully back into the saddle, shaking from head to foot.

'I don't know what I looked like,' she cried. 'But you were wonderful!'

Dancer was moving purposefully across the paddock as if to say, OK, let's move on to the next one.

'No,' Polly cried, pulling her in. 'I've got to learn how to do this properly,' she said. 'Otherwise you might get hurt and I might break my neck!'

Polly didn't get a chance to speak to Miss T. until lunch time. When she'd finished telling her what happened in the paddock, Miss T. put down her sandwich and stared at her.

'What?' she gasped. 'She jumped the cross-country course?'

'No, only one,' Polly quickly explained. 'But I'm sure she was trying to tell me that she wants to jump.'

'Those are high jumps,' Miss T. added. 'Are *you* alright?'

Polly beamed.

'I loved it!'

'We'd better talk about this later,' Miss T. said, glancing at her watch. 'I've got an idea – bring Dancer over to the school at five. Your lesson was cut short this morning, we'll finish it in private later on.'

Vida and Ella were dying to hear all about Dancer.

'Where did she come from?'

'From a woman in Whittlesford.'

'What's she like to ride?'

'Brilliant, but she's afraid of crowds.'

'Why did she freak when I came up behind her?' Toby asked.

'I think she thought you were going to whip her.'

'Has she been badly treated?'

'The farrier told Miss T. the boys she lived with knocked her about.'

Polly talked so much she hardly got a chance to open her sandwiches. Suddenly it was two o'clock and they were running in all directions,

trying to get the horses tacked up in time for
the afternoon classes.

Promptly at five Polly trotted Dancer up to the
school and found Miss T. sitting on the fence,
watching the house martins swoop in and out
of the high, timber rafters where their nests
were built. Patting Dancer she said,

'I want to see what she's like on her own.
Let's give it a whirl.' Polly looked at Miss T.,
too nervous to ask the question she'd been
pondering all day – why are you asking *me* to
ride? She knew Toby and Vida would have been
better and Jessica Pemberton would be perfect,
so why her? Seeing her puzzled expression
Miss T. answered the question for her.

'You're the right size, nice and light too, and
Dancer likes you. She jumped for you this
morning, so she might just do it again.'

Polly nodded, satisfied with the answer, and
set off at a steady trot around the school. Miss
T. worked her quickly through the diagonals
and leg changes, then after a few full circles
moved her onto the trotting poles. Polly could
feel Dancer responding. She could see her
excitement, in the set of her head and the way
her ears moved forward expectantly as Miss
T. called out to her. Suddenly confident, she
threw back her head and tossed her silver
mane. Polly knew she wanted to jump. Taking

her on an extended canter, she circled the school before bringing Dancer up to the first jump – the spread that had freaked her that morning.

'It's OK, I promise you,' she said firmly but kindly.

'Look ahead,' Miss T. called out. 'And shift your weight forward, taking all the weight on your thigh and ankle.'

Dancer took the three foot spread as if it were a playschool toy then headed with confidence and ease for the poles, planks and gate. Polly moved with her, listening to Miss T. as they took off and landed.

'Excellent, excellent. Clear round,' Miss T. enthused as Polly trotted Dancer over to her. 'You really are a star, aren't you?' Dancer tossed her head and huffed, extremely pleased with herself.

'Isn't she wonderful?' Polly spluttered, breathless with excitement.

'She certainly is,' Miss T. agreed. 'And with patience we'll get her back into the show ring, winning those trophies, won't we Dancer?' Dancer nudged Polly who had climbed down to cuddle her.

'Don't worry,' Miss T. added. 'Your friend Polly can come too!'

Chapter Nine

Grids, Flatwork and Jumps!

Her thoughts filled with Dancer, Polly started the school week in a daze of happiness. She was soon brought down to earth when Ms Johnson told her that she'd got four out of ten in her maths test. Polly was no fool. She realised that if her parents thought she was shirking her school work they'd instantly put a stop to the gardening work and that would be the end of her long-term riding plan.

'It's not fair,' she grumbled to her friends in the playground. 'Just when I was thinking life was totally perfect.'

'You'll just have to work extra hard at school this week,' Vida advised.

Polly pulled a long face.

'That's a lot easier said than done,' she said.

Tuesday and Thursday turned out to be hot afternoons. Weeding and watering Mrs Bevan's huge garden was exhausting and Polly began to feel quite dizzy under the sun's blaze.

When Mrs Bevan saw Polly's hot, red face she called her into the cool kitchen and gave her a long drink of blackcurrant juice. Polly gulped it back and was instantly refreshed.

'Thank you,' she said gratefully.

'I wonder if these might be any good to you?' Mrs Bevan said, handing over two pairs of cream-coloured jodphurs. Polly held them up against her waist.

'They look the right length and I like the style too,' she said, fingering the shaping on the hips and thighs.

'Yes, they're a bit old fashioned but they're rather nice,' Mrs Bevan said, pleased that Polly liked them. 'They belonged to my daughter who's grown up now. Do keep them if they're useful.'

'Thank you very much,' Polly said gratefully. 'I'll wear them for my next lesson.'

When she wasn't gardening after school she was doing extra school work, so there wasn't much time to call into the yard and see Dancer.

By the end of the week her efforts had paid off. She got her eight pounds from Mrs Bevan and six out of ten in their weekly maths test.

'Things are looking up,' Ella said. 'And, it's Friday, so we're all happy.'

'YEAH!' Vida and Polly cheered. 'It's Friday!'

Dancer was delighted to see Polly early on Saturday morning. She brushed her head against Polly's sleeve and nibbled her fingers as if to say, where have you been? Polly laughed at her funny little ways.

'I've missed you too, beautiful,' she said, kissing Dancer's soft head. 'Now, come on, let's get you smartened up or Miss T. will think I don't love you any more.'

As she brushed Dancer down with a body brush Polly chatted and patted her. Then she carefully combed out her flowing mane and tail, holding the silky hair up to the light and watching the sun send it into a shimmer of silver. It was such a joy to groom Dancer – she responded delicately to her every touch, enjoying the calm, gentle intimacy. Polly was only just picking out her hooves when Ella popped her head over the stable door and said,

'Get your act together. It's nearly nine.'

Polly looked up and saw Jessica Pemberton trotting by on Merlin, quickly followed by Toby on Galaxy.

'Oh, no, I've been dreaming!' she cried.

'Well stop dreaming and start tacking up,' Ella said with a laugh. 'See you up in the school.'

She trotted off on Belle, leaving Polly to quickly tack up Dancer. When she got to the school the lesson was only just underway.

'Come on, beautiful, let's show them a thing or two,' Polly whispered into Dancer's mane. Responding to her voice Dancer tossed her pretty head and trotted in as if she were the Queen of England.

'Well, good morning!' Miss T. said as Dancer frisked before her, bright-eyed and bushy-tailed.

The lesson couldn't have been more different from the week before. Dancer had a new confidence and did everything with style. Vida and Ella smiled with pleasure at the pony's high step and proud carriage, Jessica Pemberton looked very po-faced. Normally it was her Merlin who stole the show, but Moon Dancer was in no mood for taking second place that morning. Responding to Polly's hands on the reins and the gentle pressure of her heels on her sides, Dancer broke into an even canter and moved elegantly into the diagonal exercises. After half an hour's flat work they started on gridwork and Dancer worked excellently through the trotting poles, moving fluently, actively lifting her shoulders and hind legs. Vida and Ella looked well-impressed, Miss T. was clearly delighted with the change in Dancer and Jessica Pemberton was furious! When it came to doing the jumping course Polly had to hold Dancer in.

'Cool it,' she murmured. 'We have to wait our turn and we're going last, because you don't like anybody coming up behind you.'

Dancer tossed her head but waited in line, watching the other ponies with intense interest. Toby was first off, over-zealous. Too keen to beat everybody else's timing, he brought down half the course. Vida was slow but perfect. Ella started off well, then went into her usual hot-headed panic which made Miss T. quite cross and almost reduced Ella to tears. The fourth rider, a girl called Alice who was riding Cyder, suddenly got terrified and ducked out, and then came Jessica Pemberton who was flawless.

'Right, Polly, let's give her a whirl,' Miss T. called, checking her watch as the hour came to an end.

Dancer was off like a rocket. She took the first parallel bar, landed lightly and turned to face the gate. Polly felt her spirits lift as Dancer opened up beneath her. The thrill of the lift off and the pleasure of a clear landing after every jump made her blood race. She was almost sorry when it was all over. So was Moon Dancer.

'Clear round!' Miss T. cried, delighted. Dancer nudged her as if to say, please, can I have another go?

Miss T. turned to Polly and beamed.

'You did excellently. Well done.'

Polly didn't have time to answer as the next class trotted in.

'You were brilliant!' enthused Ella as they trotted back to the yard.

'What a star she is,' Vida said, admiringly.

A snooty voice from behind popped Polly's bright bubble of happiness.

'I'm surprised Miss T.'s impressed,' Jessica Pemberton said haughtily. 'You can hardly keep your seat and the pony's a wreck.'

Polly was so stunned she couldn't retort but Ella was in there like a shot.

'I trust Miss T.'s judgement a lot more than *yours*!' she snapped. Jessica stared at Ella as if she were something the cat had just dragged in then trotted off with her nose in the air.

'What a cheek!' seethed Ella, red in the face and all set for a fight.

'She's just jealous,' Vida said. 'Think about it. She's ruled the roost for years on Merlin and suddenly along comes Dancer and she's no longer the star.'

'Tough!' Ella retorted.

'It's stupid to be jealous of somebody like *me*,' Polly said. 'I'm a beginner and she's so accomplished.'

'Don't underestimate yourself, Polly,' Ella said. 'You were pretty impressive doing that jumping course.'

'Anything but a beginner,' Vida added. 'You looked like you'd been jumping for years.'

Polly blushed.

'It was Dancer, she was doing everything, not me.'

Ella gave her a friendly push.

'Polly, you were good – believe it.'

Overwhelmed by her friends' praise and generosity Polly smiled saying, 'You were pretty good too.'

'Good!' Ella almost exploded. 'I was a *disaster*! I'm OK until I see that gate and then I just turn to jelly.'

'It will get better,' Vida insisted.

'Yes, you were much better this week than last,' Polly added, then burst into a fit of giggles. 'At least you got halfway round the course this time!'

'Well, thank you!' Ella answered.

Laughing and teasing each other the girls led their ponies into the yard where they gave them water then set to, mucking out the stables. It was a long hard day, but a happy one. By five o'clock Polly was tired but still reluctant to leave.

'I'll just pop in and say good-bye to Dancer,' she called to Vida and Ella.

'Honestly, you should bring your bed over here and sleep with that pony!' Ella teased.

'If only I could,' Polly answered.

She loved to surprise Dancer, peeping over the door and catching her unawares. The sight of her burnished silver coat against the gloom of the stable reminded Polly of the very first time she had seen her. Dancer sniffed and neighed; she knew Polly was there.

'Surprise, surprise,' Polly cried.

Dancer loved Polly's visits, especially if they went with mints and the odd carrot. Miss T. was surprised to find Polly in Dancer's stable.

'Goodness, I thought you'd gone home half an hour ago,' she said.

'I'm trying to tear myself away,' Polly answered then laughed as Dancer nibbled her fingers. 'It's hard leaving her when she's having fun.'

'Polly, I've been thinking about Dancer. After her performance this morning I feel she'd benefit from doing a show. It might just remind her of how things used to be,' Miss T. patted Dancer affectionately. 'She was doing superbly as a show pony until those two wild boys in Whittlesford broke her confidence.'

'It's worth a try,' Polly answered, feeling a sudden twinge of jealousy. She was sure Miss T. would ask Jessica Pemberton to ride Dancer. It made sense, she was the best showjumper in the yard. Miss T. however had other plans. Staring thoughtfully at Polly she said,

'A show would be good experience for you too. Would you like to try the open class at Ickleton show at the end of June?'

Polly tried to speak but could only squeak.

'I know what you're going to say, you haven't had enough experience.'

Polly nodded.

'I've only had three lessons,' she blurted out.

'That's true, but you have a natural seat for jumping, you're light and wiry, perfectly co-ordinated and you've taken to jumping like a duck to water.'

Polly's face flushed so hot with excitement she thought she was going to faint.

'I'd *love* to!' she exclaimed.

'Good, I'll put you through your paces.'

'But there's a problem,' Polly said. 'I can only just afford one lesson a fortnight,' she blushed as she finished the sentence.

'We'll sort something out,' Miss T. answered briskly. 'An extra bit of tuition now and then will be payment for your work around the yard. After all, you are here a lot,' she added with a laugh.

Polly smiled. She wasn't going to argue, but nevertheless she knew that Miss T.'s offer was extremely generous.

'We'll do a few practice sessions this week,' Miss T. said as she hurried off to answer the phone ringing in her office.

Polly stared at Dancer, thunderstruck.

'I don't believe it,' she gasped. 'I'm going to a *show!*'

Dancer pawed the ground, as if to say, so am I!

Chapter Ten

Jessica Pemberton

The week that followed was one of the most
hectic of Polly's life. A combination of school,
Mrs Bevan's garden and, best of all, a half hour
practice with Miss T. on Monday afternoon.

'You'll be doing the three foot open class,'
Miss T. said. Polly's jaw dropped but Miss T.
continued in her characteristic, matter-of-fact
manner. 'Probably ten spreads, though they
might stick in a few more just for fun.'

Fun! Ten or more spreads at three foot. Who
did she think she was – superwoman?

'So, let's get down to business – your seat.

Sit deep, deep down and concentrate on your rear end. Make it heavy so that you're fused with your pony. Give it a whirl,' she said, using her favourite expression. Polly nodded and set off around the school, sitting deep, and concentrating on her rear end.

'Think bottom heavy – like a big sack of dough,' Miss T. called out.

Polly smiled but concentrated on the image, which certainly made her think *heavy*.

'And keep that strong line, from shoulder to hip to heel.'

Polly quickly corrected her position.

'Excellent. A couple of big circles around the school then on to the diagonals.'

The warm-up exercises and the flat work seemed to take forever. All Polly wanted to do was jump!

'You might think you're ready, but you're not,' Miss T. told her firmly. 'Neither is Dancer. Jumping is a gradual build-up, a co-ordinating of mind and body, for both pony and rider.'

They warmed up through trotting poles, which Miss T. crossed so that Dancer would jump straight through the centre of the jump. Dancer moved in perfect rhythm, getting the right stride and lifting her front and hind legs in a neat high step.

'OK, on to the jumps,' Miss T. called.

Dancer tossed her head, as if to say, about time too!

'Knees bent, heels down, head up, hands forward and low,' Miss T. instructed. 'Build up to a canter and approach the first fence. Head up!' she reminded Polly sharply.

The first spread, a cross, was looming. Polly collected Dancer in and put her weight well forward.

'Lift more with your thighs,' Miss T. called. 'Really take the weight off her.'

With throbbing thigh muscles Polly took the rise and landed tidily, apart from a sneak backward glance.

'Keep your head up on landing and never look back,' Miss T. called. 'Direct all your attention to the jump ahead. Anticipate, collect her in, throw your weight onto your thighs – good!'

Dancer was moving perfectly onto the next jump, the planks, but Polly fluffed it by putting her onto the wrong leg. Dancer took the jump badly and brought it down behind her.

'Look ahead!' Miss T. snapped as Polly turned to see the fallen planks.

This time Polly did exactly as instructed. Concentrating only on the double coming up she got Dancer onto her right stride, moved forward and up they went, up and over. Taking a sharp left turn, Polly headed for the wall then on a loop for the cavelleti and the gate. It was an exhilarating, totally exhausting lesson, and Polly adored it.

'You'll do fine,' Miss T. said as they finished. Dancer huffed and puffed excitedly, pushing against Miss T. demanding praise. Miss T. patted her silver-bright mane and smiled. 'You, little lady, are a star!'

The next day was Tuesday so Polly was busy after school, working in Mrs Bevan's garden, then catching up with her homework. On Wednesday she dashed to the yard straight after school and found Tom, the groom, in the office.

'Miss T.'s had to take Passadoble to the vet's in Newmarket,' Tom said. 'I've got to teach her adult class so could you mix the horses' feeds? The instructions are on the feed board in the feed room.' Polly nodded eagerly and ran off to collect the buckets. It was while she was in the feed room, measuring out the mollychaff, that Jessica Pemberton walked in. Polly looked up from the mollychaff and saw Jessica eyeing her. Seeing her cold expression she quickly glanced down and continued with what she was doing.

'I hear you're entering the open in the Ickleton Show,' Jessica said. Polly felt like saying, what's that to do with you? but remembered her manners and said, 'Miss T. suggested I should try the open on Dancer.'

'And you've been scrounging free lessons too,' Jessica added, waspishly. 'Can't your parents afford *anything*?'

Polly quickly decided it was a waste of time trying to be polite to somebody who was as rude as Jessica Pemberton.

'What my parents can afford is none of your business,' she answered. 'And I am not scrounging off Miss T. I'm having extra coaching in exchange for work I do about the yard.'

'I hope you're not stupid enough to think a few odd lessons here and there are going to make you or that neurotic wreck of a pony into a show jumping success?' Jessica sneered.

Polly stared at her, thunderstruck. Nobody had *ever* talked to her so rudely in her entire life. Clearly, for reasons best known to herself, Jessica was trying to wind her up and Polly tried very hard not to react to insults.

'If you think you're up to doing the open, why don't you and I have our own private competition here?' Jessica taunted.

Polly stopped mixing the mollychaff and gaped at her – had the girl gone mad?

'Compete with you?' she asked. 'Why?'

'Because if you're not up to my standard you certainly won't be up to competition standard,' Jessica said arrogantly.

Polly blushed. The very last thing she wanted
to do was compete with Jessica Pemberton –
at any level. She just wanted her to go away
and leave her in peace.

'Well – speak, for goodness sake!' Jessica
cried. 'We could set up a course in the school –'

She never finished the sentence. Polly
interrupted her, shocked to her boots.

'Miss T. would never allow us to set up a
jumping course for our own private purposes.'

'Of course she wouldn't and we wouldn't ask
either,' Jessica answered, as quick as a flash.
'We'd do it on Friday. I know for a fact that
Miss T.'s away for the day.'

Polly knew that too. Miss T. had told her
the day before.

'What would be the point?' Polly asked,
desperate to get out of what was turning into
a nightmare situation.

'Quite simply this – if you can't beat me
there's no way you should enter the open at
Ickleton and disgrace the good name of the
yard.'

Polly gulped and fought for self-control. She
knew it would be crazy to get into this with Jessica
but how many more of her insults could she take?

'Wimp!' Jessica mocked.

Something snapped inside Polly. She'd had
enough of being treated like a useless reject.

'I never said no,' she answered, icily. 'I just think Miss T. won't like it, particularly as I'm the one who'll be riding one of her ponies without permission.'

Jessica shrugged.

'She won't know, idiot,' she answered. 'We'll meet at four, we'll have finished by five and Miss T.'s not due back till the evening. What's your problem? Are you for it, or not?'

Polly nodded, her stomach churning with nerves.

'Right. Friday, four o'clock,' Jessica finished. 'And don't chicken out!'

The following morning Polly told Vida and Ella her news.

'What a pain that Jessica Pemberton is!' Ella exploded. 'I'd love to give her a piece of my mind.'

'She's more than a pain,' Vida said. 'She's a menace.'

'I tried to get out of it but she kept taunting me, telling me I was no good. In the end I just lost my temper and agreed.' She scuffed her feet on the playground. 'If Miss T. should find out . . .' words failed her, but not Ella.

'She'll go *crackers!*' she finished for Polly.

'Who will you ride?' Vida asked, clearly very worried.

'It'll have to be Dancer, she's the only pony I've ever jumped.'

The girls stared at each other, stunned. Suddenly Ella said, with great determination, 'Come on, think positive!'

'I can't,' Polly admitted. 'I'm too scared.'

'You have to,' Ella bossed. 'You can't get out of this mess now that you're in it, so you've got to win.'

'Beat Jessica Pemberton – come on!'

'Ella's right,' Vida interrupted. 'There's no point in doing this if you think you're going to lose – that's exactly what Jessica Pemberton wants you to do – lose.'

'She'll try and beat you on Friday so that you'll lose your bottle and give up on the open. What a schemer,' Ella added.

Polly's eyes flashed anger.

'No way,' she raged. 'No way is she doing that to *me!*' Too angry to stand still, Polly walked back and forth across the playground then suddenly stopped. Whirling round on Ella and Vida who'd been tailing her, she declared,

'I'm going to show that Jessica Pemberton what Dancer and I are made of. I'm going to beat her – if it's the last thing I do!'

Chapter Eleven

Caught in the Act

By Friday Polly was feeling sick with nerves. She'd hardly slept the night before and hadn't eaten a thing for breakfast.

'Are you ill?' her mum asked.

'I've got a headache,' Polly answered.

It wasn't a lie. She had a headache, tummy ache and worst of all – heartache. It wasn't the competition that troubled her as much as betraying Miss T. She'd been so kind and generous, given so much of her time and energy and now Polly was using one of her ponies in a crazy competition – without even asking her permission. She felt even worse after breakfast, when Miss T. phoned and said, 'Polly, I'll be away all day. Can you be sure to exercise Dancer after school?'

Polly's heart sank into her school shoes. Thank goodness Miss T. had no idea exactly what kind of exercise she was planning.

At school Vida and Ella were one hundred percent supportive.

'We'll be there,' Vida said.

'Really?' Polly gasped.

'You don't think we'd leave you alone with Jessica Pemberton?' Ella asked. 'We're going to watch her every move and make sure there's no dirty business.'

Polly threw her arms around Vida and Ella.

'You really are the two best friends I've ever, ever had.'

She was doubly grateful of their support at three forty-five that afternoon when she walked into the yard, shaking like a jelly.

'I don't think I can even tack up,' she dithered.

'Get a grip,' Ella said firmly. 'Here comes the pain-in-the-neck herself.' Jessica swanned by, leading Merlin on a lead rope.

'See you in five minutes,' she smirked.

The sight of her pale hard face did something to Polly.

'She's not going to walk all over me!'

'No way!' Ella agreed.

'Go for it!' Vida added.

Keeping a steely, determined mood they hardly spoke as they tacked up and led Dancer out of her stable.

'We'll be with you all the way,' Vida said, squeezing Polly's arm tight when they reached the school.

'Fingers crossed,' Ella said, holding up her crossed fingers and winking. 'We know you can do it.'

Strengthened and comforted by her friends' conviction, Polly trotted into the school and stopped short.

'Too much for you?' Jessica Pemberton asked, clearly delighted that Polly looked stunned by the course.

Polly shrugged and tried not to smile. How could Jessica Pemberton have known that she'd jumped almost the same course on Monday with Miss T. – and all the jumps had been at least six inches higher? Determined not to give anything away she kept her expression dead pan and started to warm up.

'We'll go for a clear round,' Jessica bossed, her snooty tone implying that she at least would make it. 'Then against the clock.'

'Aren't you going to warm up?' Polly asked, remembering Miss T.'s advice from the previous lesson – 'Jumping's a gradual build-up between rider and pony.'

'I've already done that,' Jessica snapped, cracking her whip hard against her boot and scaring Dancer.

'Well, Polly hasn't!' Ella snapped, her face bright red with anger. 'Take your time, Polly,' she called across the school in a voice not unlike Miss T.'s. 'Warm her up on the flat while Vida and I check the jumps.'

Jessica Pemberton glared at the two girls.

'Are you her bodyguards or her nanny?' she sneered.

'Neither,' Vida answered icily. 'We're her friends. Something you probably don't know much about.'

'We're here to see there's no funny business,' Ella added. 'It's bad enough that you suggested this fiasco, let's just make sure there are no *accidents,*' she stressed the word as she finished.

'If there are any accidents it'll be that one over there,' Jessica mocked as she eyed Polly nervously warming up. Whacking Merlin smartly with her heels she turned away. 'Now, if you don't mind, I'd like to warm up.'

'I thought you'd already done that,' Ella called after her.

'Don't waste your breath,' Vida said. 'Come and help me check the jumps.'

There were ten three foot jumps, starting with a gate, cross poles, planks, a couple of verticals, a parallel, a cavelleti, a pyramid and a double, ending with a wall.

'I don't fancy this,' Ella whispered.

'Neither do I,' Vida agreed. 'And from the expression on Polly's face, neither does she.'

Oddly enough it wasn't the course that was worrying Polly as much as Dancer who seemed very overwrought. She tensed every time Merlin came near her and threw back her head at the sight of Jessica Pemberton.

'I don't like her either,' Polly whispered into her mane. 'But I'm stuck with this and I'm going to win.'

Suddenly Jessica's voice rang out.

'Can we get on?' she cried. 'Otherwise Miss T. will find us here when she gets home this evening.'

Polly nodded and joined her at the starting post. Jessica Pemberton went first, off like a rocket over every jump, almost flawless. It was only at the double that Jessica nearly took a nose-dive but she corrected her position and came zipping over the final spread, her face smug and digustingly well-pleased.

'Yuk!' Ella said, hardly bothering to lower her voice.

'Your turn,' Jessica said, coming up too close to Dancer and waving her whip. It was a bad start for Dancer who shied and reared up.

'Put that thing away,' Ella cried, snatching at her whip.

Polly turned her attention to the jumps, focusing her mind and calming herself with deep, steady breathing. As Dancer felt her relax she too relaxed and the pair moved as one. Polly sat deep and heavy, as she'd been taught, and cantered towards the first jump. Dancer was over, with inches to spare, and with a quick, triumphant swish of her silver tail she headed towards the crossed poles which she took perfectly in the centre. As they approached the upright planks, Polly made the silly mistake of putting Dancer onto the wrong leg, but the bright little pony righted herself and took the jump, though it did wobble precariously as they landed. Telling herself not to look behind, Polly forged on, gaining strength and confidence with every jump. Suddenly they were coming to the wall, the last jump, and Dancer's ears went down and not up. She stopped short and Polly all but tumbled over her head. Quickly regaining her composure she took it again, slower and with less bravado, talking Dancer through it, not forcing but encouraging. Dancer tried again and soared like a bird, touching down gracefully with an excited toss of her head.

'Well done,' Polly cried, so delighted with

Dancer's courage that she'd forgotten all about Jessica Pemberton.

'Well, I suppose you could call that a clear round,' Jessica sniffed.

'It *was* a clear round,' Ella insisted. 'Dancer just lost her nerve for a second or two.'

'Well she won't be able to do that against the clock,' Jessica said. She waited for the second hand of the clock on the wall to reach twelve, then zoomed. Merlin was quick and light, taking turns nimbly and fearlessly. Polly wondered why Jessica yanked him so hard on the bit. He was such a willing, courageous little pony and did everything that she asked of him, he hardly needed his mouth pulled at every turn. All was going well until Jessica reached the cavelleti, one of the easiest jumps but she took it carelessly and brought it down. Four faults but her timing was amazing.

'Sixty-two seconds,' Jessica announced, checking the wall clock. 'Not bad.' Polly thought it was sensational until Dancer took off and then for the first time in her life she *really* knew what speed was. Dancer knew exactly what to do and how to do it. Polly instantly responded to her experience. She sat deep and moved with her, throwing her weight forward onto her thighs and toes, focusing herself constantly on the jumps ahead, never looking back, not even when the wretched planks wobbled again after their descent. She loved it. Loved the speed, the grace and Dancer's new-found confidence. The way she kicked up her hind legs after a good clearance or swished her tail as she moved into a spread. The accuracy of Dancer's timing and the precision of her jumps were breathtaking. Nothing mattered – nothing in the world. Laughing with pleasure Polly approached the double, and was just about to collect Dancer in when, to her utter horror, she saw Miss T. striding white-faced into the school. Unable to think straight, full of fear and shame, Polly lost all her concentration and control. Dancer took the jump automatically but went straight through the middle of it, bringing the lot down behind her. Polly slid straight over Dancer's head, and banged her head on the side of the upright. As Miss T. loomed over her, Polly mercifully fell into a deep faint.

Chapter Twelve

The Invalid

When Polly came round she was in her own bed at home, with a blinding headache.

'Shhhh, love, relax,' her mum said softly as Polly tried to move.

'Oh, Mum! Mum!' Polly cried, tears rolling down her cheeks. 'I was so stupid.'

'I know all about it,' Mrs Styles soothed.

'I should never have let Jessica Pemberton talk me into it,' Polly ranted. 'Oh, Mum . . .' she wept.

'It's alright now, it's over,' Mrs Styles soothed.

Suddenly Polly sat bolt upright.

'Dancer?' she gasped. 'Is she hurt?'

'No, she's fine, absolutely fine.'

'Really?' Polly asked, weak with relief.

'Promise,' Mrs Styles whispered as she softly stroked her daughter's hot forehad. 'Now try to sleep.'

Polly lay in bed for three days, concussed, bruised and extremely miserable. Her brother sat and read to her, or chatted, something rather uncharacteristic for him, but he was worried about his sister and tried to cheer her up with funny stories. As Polly got stronger Vida and Ella were allowed to visit. They dropped by with books and sweets, which they ate as they huddled round Polly's bed, gossiping.

'How's Miss T.?' Polly asked.

'Very grumpy,' Vida answered honestly.

'She really laid into us,' Ella blurted out. 'Tried to say the whole stupid idea was all our fault.'

Polly gasped.

'But it wasn't!' she cried.

'Don't worry, we soon put her straight,' Vida explained.

'We said we were there to keep an eye on you,' Ella added. 'Creepy Jessica tried saying that it was all your fault – she lied through her teeth while you were on the ground, unconscious!' she added dramatically.

'Miss T. didn't believe her for a minute but she was too busy getting you sorted out to argue,' Vida said. 'Tom called the doctor and he brought you home.'

'What a disaster,' Polly groaned.

'Yes,' Ella agreed then quickly added, 'but it does have some advantages.' She paused with a huge smile on her face. 'Jessica Pemberton's left the yard!'

'What?' Polly cried, jumping up in the air with excitement, then rubbing her throbbing forehead. 'Ouch! that hurts.'

'Lie back and we'll tell you all,' Vida promised.

Polly arranged herself on the pillows and listened, gobsmacked, to their story.

'Jessica and Miss T. had a blazing row after the doctor took you home,' Ella started. 'We heard them from the tack room.' Vida giggled.

'It was too good to miss,' she continued. 'So, we crept up and hid outside Miss T.'s office. We heard every juicy word.'

'Go on,' Polly commanded, wide-eyed with excitement.

'Well, Miss T. said she was disgusted with Jessica.'

'She said she could have killed both you and Dancer,' Ella interrupted. 'It was brilliant.'

'Jessica tried to say it was all your idea—'

'That's when I nearly popped out and thumped her,' Ella added. 'Fortunately Vida held me back or we would never have heard the end of the row.'

'Go on!' Polly cried.

'Then Jessica completely lost her rag and said the yard was full of riff-raff riders and knackered old hacks. You can imagine Miss T.'s reaction. She told Jessica if she didn't like it she could buzz off, immediately.'

'Yippee!' Polly cheered, giving herself another sharp pain in the head.

'Cool it, or your mum will throw us out,' Ella said.

'Jessica left yesterday,' Vida said, finishing the story off. 'Her mother drove Merlin off in the horse box; he seemed a bit sad,' she added, regretfully.

'He's a sweet little pony,' Polly said.

'But Jessica Pemberton's a pain in the tonsils!' Ella exploded. 'Who cares? She's gone – forever!'

Polly lay back on her pillows and let out a long sigh of relief.

'Absolutely brilliant,' she said but the smile on her face slowly faded as she grew thoughtful. 'But that doesn't exactly help me, does it?' Vida and Ella glanced at each other.

'I've let Miss T. down badly,' Polly said.

'Completely used her, in fact.'

'Just stay out of her way for a while,' Vida advised. 'She'll forget it, eventually,' she added hopefully.

Polly looked glum.

'I doubt it, but I haven't got the nerve to go into the yard so I'll be well out of her way.' She sighed heavily and tears came to her eyes. 'Oh, dear, I do miss Dancer!'

Chapter Thirteen

Future Prospects

By the middle of the week Polly was practically tearing her hair out. She couldn't go to school, even though she felt fine. The doctor had recommended that she should have the week off, to build up her strength. She couldn't do any gardening work – not that it mattered, she thought to herself. How could she ever ask to ride one of Miss T.'s ponies again? Worst of all, she hadn't seen Dancer for six days. The only good thing she could do was stand at her bedroom window and gaze into the sunny paddock where the ponies grazed all day long.

It was while she was standing at her bedroom window, staring wistfully at Belle and Rosie snuffling each other in the shade of an elderflower bush, that Miss T. walked down the lane. Polly immediately ducked behind the curtains then heard a loud knock on their front door.

'Why, Miss T.,' her mother said in a warm, welcoming voice. 'How very nice to see you. Do come in.'

Polly nearly passed out. Miss T. was standing, right this minute, in their sitting room. Suddenly there were steps on the stairs and Sam walked into her room.

'It's Miss T.,' he announced. 'She wants to see you,' he added with a wicked smile.

'Tell her I'm ill,' Polly hissed, leaping into bed, fully clothed.

Her brother burst out laughing.

'Tell her I'm dead!' Polly added, almost in tears.

'I can't. Mum's just told her you're making a good recovery.'

Polly groaned and buried her head under her duvet. When she came up for air Miss T. was standing in the doorway and Sam had disappeared. Polly threw the duvet off and tried to pull herself together.

'Oh, hello . . .' she started.

Miss T. laughed at her awkward expression.

'I just thought I'd drop by and see how you were' she said, dropping a pile of wonderful pony magazines onto the bed. Polly looked at them and smiled in delight.

'Thank you!' she cried, suddenly forgetting her nerves.

'That's alright,' Miss T. paused then added, 'Dancer's missing you.' At the mention of the pony's name Polly's eyes filled with tears.

'Dancer . . .' she murmured and unable to stop herself she burst into tears. 'Oh, Miss T. I'm so sorry!' she wept.

Miss T. smiled easily and patted Polly's shaking hands.

'Calm down, it's all over. We must look to the future,' she said. 'Dancer's lonely so you must pay her a little visit tomorrow. Not too long, your mum says you must build up your strength.'

Polly nodded and smiled.

'Five minutes would be wonderful,' she said, wiping the tears off her cheeks. 'But, but,' she dithered nervously. 'Can you ever trust me again?' she blurted out in a rush.

'Absolutely!' Miss T. answered. 'I'll tell you something. When I walked into the school and saw you jumping Dancer without my permission, or my guidance, I was furious.'

Polly blushed but Miss T. quickly carried on.

'Then I saw you take those verticals and I

was so impressed I forgot my anger. It was at that point that you saw me and panicked,' she added with a wink. 'Well, there we are,' she finished, rising to her feet. 'I must get back, there's lots to do now that I haven't got a little helper around the yard. I really must do something about it.'

With a wave she was gone, leaving Polly wide-eyed with happiness. Quickly she leapt off the bed and ran to the window. As Miss T. hurried down the path Polly called out, 'See you tomorrow morning. Give Dancer a big kiss from me!'

The following morning she was in the yard just as soon as she could escape her mum's beady eye. She flashed past Miss T.'s office, hardly stopping to call hello, and dashed across to the pony block. Creeping up, holding her breath, Polly caught Dancer unawares. Standing against the gloom of the stable she lifted her delicate head and sniffed the air. Suddenly she whinnied and tossing her mane she trotted over to the door where Polly was waiting.

'Hi there,' she whispered, burying her face against Dancer's and sniffing in the glorious perfume of her mane. 'Did anybody ever tell you you're the most beautiful little pony in the world?'

After a lot of kissing and cuddling on Polly's part, followed by even more nuzzling and nibbling from Dancer, Polly finally set to with the body brush. The minutes disappeared into an hour as Polly chatted and groomed Dancer, telling her all the news as she worked the pony's coat to a shimmering bright silver. Soon Miss T. popped her head over the door.

'Sorry to interrupt this special moment,' she said, 'but I thought you might like to see these. They've just come in the post.' Polly took the forms Miss T. gave her and studied them.

'They're for the Ickleton Show,' she said then paused, astonished to see her name written up for the open. 'Me!' she yelped. 'Me, riding Dancer.'

'It's important to back a winning team,' Miss T. answered briskly. 'You've less than a month to get into shape. Don't waste a minute of it.'

When Miss T. had gone Polly pressed her head against Dancer's smooth burnished neck and kissed her.

'We're going places,' she whispered. 'And I'm the luckiest girl in the world!'